A WINNING TRICK

JAYNE DAVIS

Verbena
Books

Copyediting & proofreading: Sue Davison

ACKNOWLEDGMENTS

Thanks to my critique partners on Scribophile for comments and suggestions, particularly Daphne and David.

Thanks also to Beta readers Barbara, Helen, Marcia, Tina and Trudy.

FOREWORD

A Winning Trick takes place three years after the events described in *Sauce for the Gander*. It is effectively an extended epilogue for that story, and not intended to be read as a standalone.

It is available free as a kindle version to readers who sign up to my newsletter. You can sign up here:

www.jaynedavisromance.co.uk/contact/

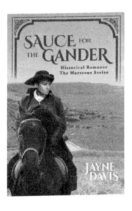

If you haven't already read *Sauce for the Gander*, you can get your copy from Amazon:

mybook.to/SauceGander

CHAPTER 1

London - Wednesday 5th April 1780

Motes of dust danced in the sunlight streaming through the window. The only sounds in the room were heavy breathing and the pad of feet as Will and Harry advanced and retreated, thrusting and parrying. After a clash of foils, Will finally managed a hit.

"Touché," Harry said, stepping back. "A fluke."

"Don't I know it." Will pulled out a handkerchief and wiped his brow, his breathing slowing. "I've had enough—it's too damned warm in here, and I'm woefully out of form." That was one of only a few hits he'd scored in this bout.

They had the practice room to themselves at this hour of the afternoon; the usual patrons of the fencing salon would be riding or driving in Hyde Park in the unexpected spring sunshine.

"Marriage is turning you soft," Harry said.

"Far from it," Will replied, refusing to take offence at his friend's needling. "I'll lay you odds I can still outshoot you. But I've no-one to fence with in Devonshire. Come and stay for a few weeks, and I'll soon be back in form."

"You can't stay in Town longer?" Harry put his foil back in the rack and picked up his coat.

Will shook his head. "My business is nearly finished, and I've been away from Connie and the girls for over a week."

"Under the cat's foot," Harry muttered, just loud enough for Will to hear.

"You should try it, you might find you like it." Will shrugged into his coat. "And you can stop baiting me—I'm not going to rise to it."

"Mama invites you to dinner this evening," Harry said as they left the building. "In fact, why don't you come over now, instead of going back to your club?"

"Thanks, I will."

"So I can beat you at billiards, too."

Will aimed a playful blow at Harry, and the two friends set off down the street. Clouds were gathering, and the air felt moist. Hopefully they'd reach Wimpole Street before the next heavy shower.

Will watched in satisfaction as his cue ball sent the red rolling directly for the end pocket. "Three points. I win."

Harry laid his cue on the table with a sigh. "Looks like you've got your revenge already, Will."

"I do have a billiards room at Ashton Tracey, and Connie knows how to—"

He broke off as Lady Tregarth walked in. "Harry, this... Hello, Will, I didn't know you were here already." She smiled, the laughter lines around her eyes deepening.

Will made his bow. "Good day, Lady Tregarth. Thank you for the invitation to dinner."

"You're always welcome here, you know that." Lady Tregarth turned to her son, holding out a folded paper.

"Harry, this letter is for you. I opened it because it was addressed to me. It is very… strange."

Harry quickly scanned down to the bottom of the sheet, his brows rising as he read the signature. "It appears to be from your wife, Will."

"What?" Will leaned over and glanced at the sheet. "That's not Connie's hand."

The puzzlement on Harry's face turned to anger as he read it properly. "This is some kind of bad joke," he said, holding the letter out to Will. "It says you're ill at home, and asks me to hurry there as soon as possible."

"Me?" Will examined the writing more closely and frowned. "It could be from Bella."

"Your sister?"

"My youngest sister, yes. What on earth…?" He shook his head. "Something's not right here."

"If it is a joke, it's a cruel one," Lady Tregarth said. "If you had not been here, Harry would have been worried. Very worried indeed, as would I."

"Would your sister do that kind of thing?" Harry asked. "And why was it addressed to Mama?"

"The staff at Marstone Park would have given any letter addressed to a man straight to my father," Will said. "This kind of thing doesn't seem like Bella, though. I'd better go home in case there is something wrong."

"You were only going to stay a couple more days, weren't you?" Harry said. "Not too great an imposition, then. Shall I accompany you?"

"You're going to dignify this… deception… by obeying?" Will waved the letter.

"Curiosity, old man. Should we ride *ventre a terre* to your bed of sickness, do you think? I'd hate you to be late for your own death."

"Harry!" his mother said. "This is no joking matter!"

3

"No, it's not," Will said. "There *is* something wrong, but not illness or accident, I think. If something was wrong at Marstone Park, Miss Glover—the governess—would have written. The letter would have gone to Ashton Tracey, but Connie would have sent any urgent letter on." He folded the letter and tucked it into a pocket. "I ought to go."

"Is this connected with Marstone being in Town, perhaps?" Lady Tregarth asked.

"I didn't know he was here, my lady," Will said. "I do not follow my father's movements."

"Sir John mentioned it the other day. On some matter of business, he said."

"It's possible, I suppose. Hopefully there'll be some news at home."

"We should set off in the morning," Harry suggested. "Too late to start now."

"Tomorrow afternoon," Will said. "I need to see Talbot before I leave."

"Take the post-chaise, if you wish," Lady Tregarth offered. "It will be more comfortable than riding in this changeable weather. Dinner will be served in a couple of hours."

"Thank you, Mama. That leaves plenty of time for me to get my revenge on Will." Harry placed the red ball on the spot again.

Ashton Tracey, Devonshire - Friday 7th April

"Go to sleep, Etta," Connie said, tucking the cover over her daughter again.

"Want story," Henrietta insisted, even though her eyes were closing.

"Not tonight." Connie had read the story twice already this evening, and countless times before. At not yet two years old, Henrietta didn't understand most of it, but still wanted to hear it again. Perhaps Connie should try reading the laundry list for a change.

"Goodnight, Etta." She dropped a kiss on Henrietta's forehead and stood, spying the butler waiting in the open doorway. Stepping out into the passage, she pulled the door to behind her. "Is something wrong, Warren?"

"No, my lady, but you have a visitor. A Miss Glover."

Glover? The name sounded vaguely familiar. Something to do with Will's sisters?

"Who is she, Warren?"

"She appears to be a gentlewoman, my lady. She asked for Lord Wingrave first, but did not state her business. I have put her in the parlour and ordered refreshments."

Warren approved of their visitor, then. "I'll be down in a few minutes."

"Very well, my lady."

Connie put her head into the next room; all was quiet from the cradle. Sukey set aside her knitting and came over to the door. "Miss Sarah's sleeping now, my lady. I rubbed some oil of cloves on her gum, it seemed to settle her."

"Thank you, Sukey. Goodnight."

Miss Glover stood as Connie entered the parlour. She looked to be about thirty years of age, although the tired lines on her face could be making her look older than her years. Her gown was a sober blue, dusty around the hem. A few tendrils of blonde hair escaped from beneath a cap, and grey eyes met Connie's in a direct gaze.

"Do sit, Miss Glover. How may I help you?"

Miss Glover sat with her back stiff, tension evident in the tight clasp of her hands in her lap. "I hoped to see Lord Wingrave, my lady. I am—I *was*—governess to his sisters."

Of course, that's why the name was familiar. After Will's

father discovered that Will had outwitted him and now owned Ashton Tracey himself, the earl had attempted to cut off all communication between the siblings. Will sent letters to his sisters via a Mr Glover in Cambridge, who forwarded them to the governess.

"Did Lord Marstone discover you have been passing letters on?"

To Connie's surprise, Miss Glover smiled, although her posture did not relax. "No, my lady, that is still a secret—although of little matter now I have been turned off."

"Without a character, I assume?"

Miss Glover nodded.

"Do not worry, Miss Glover. We will help you find another position."

"Thank you, my lady. Lord Wingrave did promise to do that if my subterfuge with the letters were ever discovered. I was hoping he would still do so in my current circumstances. However that isn't the sole reason I came here; I need to tell Lord Wingrave about the earl's plan for his sisters."

That sounded ominous. "He is away from home at the moment, and not expected back for several days yet."

Miss Glover's brow creased. "I… It is quite urgent that I talk to him, my lady. Could I trouble—?" She broke off at a knock on the door. Barton entered with a tray and set out tea and a plate of biscuits on a table between their chairs.

"Thank you, Barton," Connie said. "Please ask Mrs Hunt to prepare a room for Miss Glover, and do not disturb us unless there is anything urgent."

"Yes, my lady."

Connie waited until the footman had left, busying herself with the tea things. "If you have just travelled from Marstone Park, Miss Glover, you must be exhausted. You must stay here, of course, until we have decided what is to be done."

She poured, and passed a cup to the governess, along with the biscuits. "Why were you turned off?"

Miss Glover took the proffered cup. "The earl has arranged a marriage for Lady Theresa, and is planning one for Lady Elizabeth. To men they have never met. The young ladies attempted to come here, my lady, and I was blamed for allowing it."

Connie sighed. She knew Will wanted to ensure his sisters had some choice of marriage partner. "You did right to come here, Miss Glover. *Did* you allow the girls to run away?"

"No. I knew nothing about it. Luckily one of the grooms saw them walking into Eversham, carrying a valise each. Lord Marstone is in London, but the groom told his lordship's steward. They were brought back before they had a chance to hire a carriage to St Albans. I got an account from them before I was turned off."

"They were planning to travel on the stage? Alone?" From St Albans they would have had to go into London to take the Exeter stage. Connie cringed at the misfortunes that could have befallen them at a busy coaching inn, or at the many stops on the way to Exeter. Their reputations would have been ruined, if nothing else. "Thank goodness they didn't get as far as London."

"Yes, indeed. They had planned their route, but I think had no idea of the possible dangers of travelling without an escort, and at their age, too."

Connie eyed the plate of biscuits; Miss Glover had eaten half of them already. She must have had a tiring journey—the details could wait until she was more rested. "Do have some more tea, Miss Glover." While the governess helped herself, Connie pulled the bell. When Barton came she asked him to have dinner put forward.

"Miss Glover, there is little we can do on this matter

today, short of sending a letter to my husband. May I suggest that you settle into your room, then join me for dinner in half an hour?" Mrs Curnow should be able to produce something in that time; she would apologise to the cook for the short notice later.

"I… Yes. Thank you, my lady."

CHAPTER 2

"I hope you found your room comfortable?" Connie asked as she took her seat opposite Miss Glover.

"Yes, thank you my lady. Indeed, I am not used to such large quarters." Miss Glover eyed the dishes set out on the dining table with appreciation. "Nor to such fare, save at home at Christmas time!"

Connie laughed. "We don't normally require such a choice ourselves, but our cook enjoys showing her talents when we have guests." She turned her head. "Barton, we will serve ourselves, thank you."

The footman left, and Connie pushed a raised pie towards her guest. "Mrs Curnow makes excellent pastry."

Miss Glover served herself a generous portion, adding a good helping of roast vegetables and chicken breast. Glancing up, she met Connie's eye and blushed.

"I gather the stage coach did not stop long for meals," Connie smiled, hoping to set the governess at her ease.

Miss Glover shook her head. "No, and when it did, there were so many people trying to get a meal at once that I hardly had time to eat. I have never travelled quite so far."

Connie let her eat a few mouthfuls before turning to the main business. "You said Lord Marstone had marriage plans for his daughters. How old are they now?"

"The twins are eighteen next month. Lady Isabella is fifteen."

"It must be time for Theresa and Elizabeth to have a season, surely?"

"Yes, but I think Lord Marstone was hoping to avoid the inconvenience," Miss Glover said. "Not to mention the possibility of the young ladies being tempted by men from unsuitable backgrounds." She took a sip of wine, before continuing. "The girls received a letter from him—from his secretary, on his behalf, that is, he did not even bother to sign it himself." She took a deep breath. "I'm sorry, my lady, it is not my place to—"

"Feel free, Miss Glover. I'm sure you are aware there is little love lost between my husband and his father."

"Even so." Miss Glover shook her head. "The letter announced Lady Theresa's betrothal to Lord Drayton, and that arrangements were also being made for Lady Elizabeth's marriage."

"And Lady Theresa has never met Lord Drayton?"

"No, my lady. I don't see how a marriage can—" Miss Glover bit her lip and looked away, her cheeks reddening. "I beg your pardon, my lady, I meant no criticism of your... I mean, I—"

"I have taken no offence, Miss Glover," Connie interrupted before the governess' words became even more entangled. "Lord Wingrave and I are lucky that a marriage arranged without consideration for the wishes of either party has turned out well. Such good fortune, for one sister, let alone both, would be too much to hope for."

"That is why I wanted to see Lord Wingrave, my lady. The girls are to go to London..." Her gaze became unfocused.

"Tomorrow, I think. As yet there has been no public announcement. Once that happens it will be too late."

"At least, too late without causing a huge scandal," Connie added.

"Exactly."

"Perhaps Lady Theresa will like Lord Drayton when she meets him?"

"It is possible, my lady, but the age difference is considerable. We looked him up in a peerage—he's over thirty, and heir to the Marquess of Bedwith, but we know no more about him than that."

"An age difference is not necessarily a bad thing," Connie pointed out.

Miss Glover sighed. "That is true. I also have to remind myself that my ideal for a husband is not every woman's."

"What *are* your requirements, Miss Glover?" Connie was intrigued.

"Mutual affection and respect, at a minimum. Someone with wide interests." The governess took a deep breath. "That is more likely to happen within my own class than yours, I realise, my lady. Even so, it does not seem right to make a betrothal when the two people have not met. Theresa is not intellectual, but the affection and respect I spoke of—surely they are desirable for *any* marriage?"

"Indeed they are. After dinner, I will write a letter to my husband. Then we may look through the newspapers to see if Lord Drayton or his father are mentioned—if anything is to be done, we will need more information."

Connie liked this woman: her willingness to give an honest opinion, and the fact that she had travelled all this way on behalf of Will's sisters. "Your family is in Cambridge, I understand?"

"Yes, my father is a lecturer at the university. I have seven brothers and sisters, all but one younger than me. I do not *have* to earn my living, my lady, but it seemed preferable to remaining at home with Mama."

Now she was rested, Miss Glover looked younger than Connie had first thought. "How old are you, Miss Glover? If you don't mind my asking."

"Twenty-five." She looked Connie square in the face. "You are wondering, I suppose, why I have not married, coming from a town with such a large population of young men?"

Connie felt her cheeks heat. It was none of her business, and Miss Glover was not being interviewed for a position. "I'm afraid I was." To her relief, her guest did not appear to have taken offence.

"It is a fair question. Many of the well-off young men seemed to regard females of my station and below as momentary diversions, and the more serious ones were either too focused on their studies or without the means to support a family."

"Whereas I would have dwindled into an unpaid house-keeper for my father, never meeting any suitable men at all, had not Marstone suddenly required a wife for his son." Connie saw Miss Glover's eyes widen at this confidence. "Miss Glover, I feel we have much in common and could be friends. Please call me Connie."

Miss Glover blushed. "I... If you wish it, my... Connie. My name is Kate. Katherine, that is, but I am called Kate by my friends."

"You wished to see me, my lady?" Archer entered the library and stood by the door.

"Yes, please come in." Connie waited until the stable manager took a seat. "I need you to send someone with an urgent message to Lord Wingrave in London. I hope it will reach him before he sets out to return here. He's staying at the Janus club." She saw Archer glance at the clock. "Not now, but first thing in the morning."

"I could take it myself, my lady."

"There's no need for you to…" Connie's words tailed off as she saw his change of expression—well hidden, but not quite suppressed. "Do you *want* to take it?"

Archer nodded, with a small smile. "Makes a change from routine, my lady."

"Very well, thank you. Warren will give you enough money for the journey, and I'll send Barton with the note when it's ready." She hesitated before carrying on, but Archer was Will's most trusted member of staff. "It is news about Lord Wingrave's sisters that he will want to know as soon as possible. If he's not at his club, enquire at Sir John Tregarth's house in Wimpole Street."

"Very well, my lady."

"He is trustworthy?" Kate asked, when Archer had gone.

"Eminently." Connie stood, going over to one of the cupboards beneath the bottom row of bookshelves. Opening the door, she took out a pile of newspapers.

"I don't know whether we will find anything in these," she said, "but we could spend a little time looking."

"The marriage could be solely about status," Kate said, but she took several of the newspapers.

"Or making a political alliance?" Connie suggested. "Does Marstone involve himself in politics?"

"He does take his seat in parliament, yes."

"Well, if we scan the parliamentary proceedings we may come across some reference to Lord Bedwith, at least." Connie took her own pile of papers back to her chair. "We will spend half an hour or so, Kate, then perhaps you will wish to borrow something to read while I write my letter?" Connie smiled as Kate's eyes lit up—a woman after her own heart.

. . .

In her letter, Connie summarised what Kate had told her, then hesitated. Should she offer to go to London herself?

Even if the suitors Marstone had picked were decent men, Will would want the girls to have a choice. That meant it wasn't just a matter of extricating Will's sisters from their proposed marriages, but of doing it without damaging their reputations. She knew little of society, but people were much the same everywhere when it came to gossip. Will would have to deal with any talk in the men's clubs, but women gossiped too. There might be something she could do, as Will's wife.

The need to go into society was something she'd worried about when she was first married and Will had mentioned looking after his sisters. Since then they'd entertained the local gentry and attended assemblies in Exeter and Bath. London society was a much more fearsome prospect.

But it had to be done. She dipped her pen into the ink and added another paragraph to the letter.

omerset - Saturday 8th April
"Last change of horses coming up in Yeovil."
Will threw down the paper he'd been trying to read and
stretched his arms. "We can stop there for refreshment, if
you wish."

"I have to say you're bearing up very well for someone on
his deathbed," Harry said.

"Do you never tire of saying—?" Will leaned forward
suddenly, peering behind the post-chaise, then dropped the
window and leaned out. He recognised that rider, surely?
"Stop the coach! Stop now!"

The carriage lurched to a halt, and Will leapt down. The
rider had disappeared around a bend in the road.

"Will, what are you doing?"

Ignoring Harry, Will reached back into the carriage. He
pulled the pistol from its holder beside the door and fired it
into the air.

"Bloody hell, Will!" Harry's voice drowned out the
swearing from the coachman as he attempted to calm the
horses.

"That was Archer riding past, I'm sure," Will said. "If it was, he'll not be able to resist coming back to see what's happening."

Harry climbed out and stood beside him.

"There, see?" Will waved an arm, and the approaching rider broke into a canter.

"Well, I'll be damned."

Archer reined in and dismounted. "My lord!" He reached into a pocket and held out a letter. "My lady sent me with this."

"What is wrong, Archer? The children?" Will could not keep the sudden anxiety from his voice.

"All are well, my lord. This is about your sisters, I understand."

Will broke the seal, and read Connie's succinct explanation. Damn Marstone—still dictating the futures of his children with no reference to their happiness. He thrust the letter at Harry and pulled his wig off, running his hand through his hair. He could only help his sisters in London, but he was so close to home now. Go on or go back?

Miss Glover might know more than Connie had written, and there was this mysterious letter of Bella's too. He needed to find out what that was about.

Onwards, then.

"Connie will be returning to London with us?" Harry asked, handing the letter back. "I'm sure Mama won't mind if you stay with us."

"And the girls and their nursemaid? She won't leave them behind."

Harry shrugged. "Mama will probably enjoy it. She goes to see Susannah and her brats often enough. And nags me to start a family," he added under his breath.

Lady Tregarth might be able to find somewhere for them to stay, at least. And Talbot—the spymaster—might have some useful information on Drayton. "Archer, tie your horse on the back and get up next to the coachman. I want you to go on to London, but I need to write some letters for you to take. We'll stop at an inn in Yeovil."

"Right you are, my lord."

"What are you thinking, Will?" Harry asked as the carriage set off again. "Mama will help, if she can. Father, too, if it won't interfere with his government business."

"Can you write to Lady Tregarth and explain? I think Archer should be able to get changes of horse tomorrow if he explains he has an urgent message, and we can set out again with the carriage on Monday."

"I'll do that, yes," Harry said.

"Archer can talk to the servants at Marstone House, find out from them as much as he can."

"Spying on your own family now?" Harry's grin showed he was still finding the situation amusing.

"You'd do the same if you had a father like mine," Will said. "It's not funny, Harry. The men Marstone has chosen *may* turn out to be adequate husbands, but would you wish your sister to be forced into marriage in this way?"

"Sorry, Will. I'll do what I can, of course."

Ashton Tracey

The afternoon had turned sunny, and despite a brisk breeze from the sea, Connie was warm enough in a sheltered spot on the terrace. Kate sat beside her, engrossed in the anonymous novel that everyone suspected was written by the Duchess of Devonshire. She'd explained that novels were not allowed at Marstone Park, and she hadn't cared to risk her job by smuggling them in.

Connie, remembering her own subterfuges before her marriage, sympathised. She couldn't settle to reading herself, her mind on what they could do to help Theresa and Elizabeth. Lizzie, Will called her. She kept her hands busy embroidering a pattern of roses on a cap for Sarah.

Archer would take two days to get to London, assuming he was sensible and stopped overnight somewhere. That meant four days before a reply could arrive. In the meantime she should think about what she would need for the trip, so she could be ready to set off at once if Will did ask her to join him.

She snipped off the pink thread and picked through the tangle of silks in her embroidery box, looking for shades of green for the leaves. A movement caught the corner of her eye—a carriage emerging from the band of trees that bordered the estate to the west.

Will? But he'd ridden to London. Then one of the passengers stuck his head out of the window and waved at her.

It *was* Will!

Will saw Connie hurrying to the top of the steps. As soon as the carriage came to a halt he jumped out and dashed up to her, giving her a big hug.

"I missed you," he said into her hair, breathing her scent of roses.

"Will?" She pushed on his shoulders so she could look into his face. "Why are you back early?"

"I'll tell you later," he said. "We met Archer just outside Yeovil, I've sent him on to London. All is well here, Connie?"

"Yes, Will. Oh, you've brought Harry with you." She dropped his hands and went over to greet Harry as Barton collected Will's saddle bags and Harry's small valise.

Will had noticed the other woman sitting with Connie; now he took a closer look. He'd only met the girls' governess a couple of times, just before his marriage, but he recognised her now. She was standing to one side, her expression uncertain.

"Miss Glover. Thank you for coming with your news." He would make sure she was reimbursed for the journey, at the very least.

"Thank you, my lord. Lady Wingrave has made me very welcome."

"If you will give me half an hour, you may tell me all the details."

Inside, he was greeted with a shriek from the upper landing. "Papa!" For such a small body, Henrietta had an exceedingly loud voice. Will sprinted up the staircase to his elder daughter, who was prevented from hurling herself down the stairs only by Sukey's grip on her leading strings.

"Hello, Poppet." He swung her up into the air, the shrieks and laughing smile bringing a big grin to his own face. "Now be a good girl for Sukey. I need to talk to Mama, then I'll come and see you."

"Sorry, my lord, she heard you come in, and—"

"No matter, Sukey." He set Henrietta down again and ruffled her hair. "I'm always happy to see my little girl." He winked at Henrietta and waited until Sukey had led her away.

Downstairs, the others had retreated to the parlour. Harry raised his brows as Will entered, one hand on the arm of his chair with his thumb pressing into the damask fabric.

"Your time will come," Will muttered as he sat next to his friend. He didn't think his life was under the thumb, but even if it was, he had no complaints.

CHAPTER 4

"Thank you, Miss Glover," Will said as the governess finished her tale. She'd related little more than Connie had written in her letter. For once, he was grateful for the way his father had all the servants reporting on his offspring. He didn't like to think what could have happened to his sisters if they'd managed to get further than the nearest village.

"We looked in the newspapers here," Connie said. "We found only a couple of references to Drayton's father, the marquess, but it seems he inclines to the Whigs in parliament. There was nothing about Drayton himself."

"That betrothal is for status, then, not political influence," Will said. "My father's interests are with the Tory Party."

"Not money?" Connie asked.

"Marstone isn't short of money, but the status of the family has always been more important to him. He'd increase that by having a daughter married to a future marquess."

"Why would Lord Drayton accept a wife, unseen?" Connie asked.

"Could be similar to your situation, Will," Harry

suggested. "His father might be nagging him to secure the succession."

"We've got a peerage somewhere," Connie said. She walked to the door, and Will heard her talking to Warren.

"A girl who has not been in society will be easily moulded to Drayton's requirements in a wife," Will added. He noticed Miss Glover's sudden frown. "That is not *my* opinion, Miss Glover, but if you've had any dealings with my father you'll know that's how he thinks. It's possible Drayton, or his father, does too."

"My apologies, my lord. I have been fortunate—" She bit her lip, and her face reddened.

"Fortunate not to have much contact with Marstone?" Will chuckled as the governess nodded. "That is a sentiment we all share. And I am very grateful to you for helping my letters to get through."

"Thank you, my lord."

"Miss Glover, you know my sisters far better than I do. That would probably be the case even if I'd managed to see them in the last few years. I have no idea yet how I can prevent my father committing Theresa to this marriage before she has a chance to find out whether or not she would be happy with Drayton, but your advice will be very helpful. Are you are willing to remain with us for a while?"

"We will take you as far as London even if you don't wish to stay with us, Kate," Connie put in. "And send you on to Cambridge with a reference."

Warren entered and handed a book to Connie. "The peerage, my lady."

"Thank you." Connie flicked through it, then passed it to Will open at the correct page. "No direct male heirs beyond Drayton," she said.

Will checked the entry. "And the marquess has no brother

—the title could go to a distant cousin." That could explain Drayton's motivation.

He closed the book, rather more firmly than necessary. Theresa deserved some choice in her future life, and he would do his best to give her that.

"Why are you back early, Will?" Connie asked. "And with Harry?"

"This arrived for Lady Tregarth," Will said, handing her the letter. "I think it's Bella's handwriting."

Connie's brows rose as she read, then she handed it to Miss Glover.

"It *is* Lady Isabella's writing," the governess said. As Will watched, she shook her head. "Oh, dear."

"Do you have some idea what this is about?" Connie asked.

"Only from overhearing some of their conversations." Miss Glover's gaze flicked towards Harry. "I heard Lady Isabella teasing Lady Theresa about… about Mr Tregarth."

"Me? I haven't seen your sisters for years, Will."

"Theresa and Lizzie used to follow us around when we played here," Will said. And a damned nuisance they'd been, too—always complaining because they couldn't keep up, or that their clothes would get dirty.

"So Bella tried to play Cupid and get Harry here to meet Theresa?" Connie shook her head, but her lips curved with amusement. "An ambitious plan, if doomed from the start."

"And rather cruel," Miss Glover pointed out. "How embarrassing for Lady Theresa if they *had* managed to reach here. Not to mention telling Mr Tregarth you were ill."

"Are you *sure* the girls haven't been reading novels, Kate?" Connie asked, still clearly amused.

It was an ill-thought through plan, but Bella was only fifteen. He'd been no better at that age. "Never mind that now," he said, before Miss Glover could reply. "We need to gather information." He tapped his finger on the peerage. "We still have only speculation about Marstone's motives in arranging this. I sent a note on with Archer asking an acquaintance if he could find some information on Drayton for me."

"We cannot set off until Monday," Connie added. "We have plenty of time to think about it. Do either of you need to stretch your legs after your journey? We could walk up to the cliffs?"

Will awaited her as Connie returned to the hall wearing her redingote. "Shall we take Etta?" he asked.

"Only if you want to take an hour or more to get there," Connie said. "She played in the orchard this morning."

"Very well—I'll have you to myself then." He bent towards her, and her breath hitched as his eyes focused on her lips. Then a clatter of boots announced Harry's arrival, ready to go. "Later," Will whispered.

"Kate's already waiting outside," Connie said, taking his arm. She was looking forward to 'later'.

They set off across the park, Harry ahead of them with Kate on his arm. From the snatches of conversation Connie heard, they seemed to be exchanging the usual pleasantries about the weather, and how this part of Devonshire differed from their own homes. For herself, Connie was content to walk in silence, breathing the fresh air and enjoying the solid warmth of Will beside her. When they reached the cliff-top she sat on a rock next to Will, snuggling close against him as he put one arm around her shoulders.

Kate's reaction, as she went to stand near the edge, reminded Connie of her own when Will first brought her here. Her face was alight with pleasure as she gazed over the white-capped waves, and watched the soaring gulls. Now she was rested, with her message delivered, the lines of tiredness had left her face and she looked more relaxed. Pretty, with her face still slightly flushed from the exercise, and a few strands of blond hair blowing in the wind. She turned to Harry, standing nearby. Connie couldn't catch her words, but from her gestures she was asking about the birds.

Will laughed; he was watching them too. "I know what Harry feels like. Your Kate is finding all the gaps in his knowledge. It took me days with the bird book before I could identify them all."

"Go and help him out, Will," Connie said. Will laughed again, and joined their guests on the cliff edge.

～

"Did your trip go well?" Connie asked, walking into Will's room with a robe over her chemise. She sat on the edge of the bed, hairbrush in hand. "Until you got Bella's letter, at least."

"Very well." Will untied his cravat, dropping it over the back of a chair. "Talbot wants to send men to Spain. I imagine he had his spies there anyway, but getting them in and out is a little more difficult now we're at war. He's suggested that we—that is Roberts, officially—get a larger vessel that will cope with weather beyond the Channel." He dropped his waistcoat on top of the cravat and unbuttoned his shirt. "He also told me he's finalised the matter of the traitor who started us off on this clandestine business."

"That's good." Although Will had reassured her that there would be no threat to them personally from the traitor who was passing government information, Connie had never quite believed him.

"Talbot said he'd used the man to pass along as much misinformation as he thought he could get away with."

"Unusual." They had rarely been told anything beyond when to expect a passenger and where he was to be taken to or collected from.

"Indeed—I'm not sure why. He wouldn't tell me who it was, although it should be quite easy to work out from what he said, should we wish to."

"Tell me the rest, Will!" She refused to let herself get distracted as he unbuttoned his breeches and pushed them down.

"He made a deal with the traitor, who sadly drowned shortly afterwards when his horse slipped on a riverbank."

Connie took a deep breath, her mind now sharply focused on Will's words, not his body. She knew, of course, that spies from both sides risked their lives, but it did not often come to her direct notice like this.

"It's a better end than a public trial and hanging, Connie," Will said, his voice quiet. "Better than he deserves, certainly. But his family had nothing to do with his traitorous activities, and this way they are not shamed."

"And Talbot doesn't have to admit to a breach of his own security," Connie added. She suspected that regard for the traitor's family had had little to do with Talbot's decision.

Will dropped his shirt over the back of a chair and picked up her hairbrush. Connie turned sideways a little as the mattress behind her sank under his weight. He ran his fingers through her hair, then began to brush it, the long strokes comforting and familiar and the occasional touches of his hands on her shoulders a promise for more intimate contact soon.

Her mind returned to their forthcoming trip. She and Will had left the girls for a few days at a time, on trips to Salisbury, Winchester, and Bath, but London was much further away. She wasn't going to leave them behind this time.

"We will take the girls with us to London, of course," she said, twisting round to face him.

One corner of his mouth lifted. "It would be simpler not to." His smile widened. "But as I've little hope of persuading you to come without them, yes, we will take them. That's one reason I carried on here with Tregarth's carriage—the girls, Nanny Swift, and Sukey, I imagine?"

"I was thinking of asking Miss Glover to help with the girls if Sukey and I cannot manage between us. Nanny deserves a few weeks holiday."

"If you think that's best, by all means." He turned her head gently and continued brushing her hair.

"I like Kate," Connie went on. "No doubt you'll be out and about in London much more than I will need to be. She will be good company." They could go to bookshops and museums together. Perhaps this trip to Town might not be so bad after all.

"Lady Tregarth will be good company, too," Will said. "She'll help if you—we—need to go into society."

"I know Harry said we'd be welcome to stay there, Will, but are you sure she won't mind?"

"I'm sure." Will put the brush down. "We've all day tomorrow to sort out the details, Connie." He cupped her face in his hands, bending towards her. "I think we should concentrate on other things for now."

"That's a good idea," she whispered, lifting her lips to his. Her heart accelerated, and all thoughts of London were forgotten.

CHAPTER 5

*S*unday *9th April*

The next morning Will spent an hour before breakfast in the nursery, helping Sarah play with her building blocks, then reading to Henrietta. Perhaps if the weather cleared up later, he'd take Henrietta to the cliffs—if he gave her a ride on his shoulders, he might not be required to wait while she investigated every worm and pebble on the way.

"So, what's the plan?" Harry asked, once the footman had laid out the breakfast things and been dismissed from the parlour.

"That depends on what we can find out about Drayton," Will said.

"And whoever your father has lined up for Elizabeth," Connie added. "I don't suppose it is worth trying to persuade your father to let them have a season first, at least."

"Asking him to do so is likely to make him even more determined on his current course of action," Will said.

"If we are all going to be in Town, you should call on

him," Connie suggested. "Things would be easier for your sisters if you were on speaking terms."

"The estrangement is not of my doing..." Will's voice tailed off as he met Connie's gaze. "Not recently, at least. If he still resents my buying Ashton Tracey, there's not a lot I can do about that. I did write to him when Henrietta was born, and again for Sarah."

Kate cleared her throat. "From what I've heard..." She glanced uneasily between Will and Connie.

"Do go on, Miss Glover," Will urged.

"This is from servants' gossip, you understand?" Kate waited for Will's nod before continuing. "When he received your letter about Henrietta, he flew into a rage. He seemed to think you'd had a daughter deliberately, just to spite him."

Will shook his head. His father was getting worse—hopefully that response had been bad temper, rather than truly believing such an impossibility. But all the more reason for not relying on his father's judgement of suitable husband material.

"Since your father cannot be influenced," Connie said, "I suppose you have to try to persuade the men to withdraw, temporarily at least. It's possible they may suit, if the girls can get to know them properly first."

"Possible, yes, but I'm not sure it's probable. If they're willing to marry my sisters without even meeting them, they're not likely to be looking for affection or liking in their wives." He smiled at Connie. "I doubt my father will make a good decision *three* times."

"I do not think any of your sisters will thrive without some affection," Kate said. "They have each other at the moment, but to send them off alone with a stranger..." She shook her head.

That wasn't going to happen if he could help it. Perhaps

Connie was right, too—he should at least try to get back on speaking terms with his father.

"So we need to find out more about them," Harry said. "Find their weaknesses, work on those to persuade them to listen."

"You talked about money and political influence last night," Kate put in. "Are your political leanings the same as your father's?"

"No." Will caught Connie's smile. "*Not* just because I don't get on with my father, madam wife!"

Connie held up her hands. "I would never suggest such a thing!"

She didn't need to, her expression had been clear enough. "Returning to the subject—any political alliance achieved by marrying off Lizzie would only last as long as my father."

"You need to start by making the acquaintance of Drayton then," Connie said. "It would be better if he didn't think you were warning him off."

"Could Drayton be doing this for a dowry as well as needing an heir?" Harry asked. "Men who need rich wives are often gamblers—unsuccessful ones."

If Drayton was a gambler, winning money from him would not of itself achieve his aim but it could provide a way in. It would have to be a game of skill, not chance.

"Anyone for a game of whist?"

Monday 10th April

Connie found Will in the library, pacing up and down. She'd seen the groom he'd sent to Exeter return, without the coach he'd gone to hire.

"The coach won't be here until midday," Will said. "We won't be in London until Wednesday evening at this rate, or later if we have any problems on the way. What if father's already exchanged—?"

"Will." Connie waited until he turned to face her. "Go on ahead—take Sir John's post-chaise if you wish. You can be there tomorrow."

"But there are too many of you for the coach, and I'm not letting you go unescorted, there's too much danger of highwaymen."

"We'll fit if Harry rides, and he'll be a perfectly good escort. We'll have Barton with us as well."

Will gazed at her, clearly torn.

"Will, you have a duty to your sisters as well as us, and their need is urgent. Or don't you trust Harry?"

"Of course I trust him!"

"Well, then?"

He pulled her close for a hug. "Thank you. I'll get the horses put to, and—"

"*I'll* give the order for the horses, you go and check with Harry."

The rest of the party finally got underway at one o'clock. Thankfully Henrietta was fascinated by the passing scenery for the first half hour, then went to sleep curled up on the seat, her head resting on Connie's lap. On the opposite seat Kate was immersed in a book, with baby Sarah burbling in a basket beside her. Sukey, never having travelled this way before, gazed eagerly out of the windows and asked Connie questions she couldn't answer about the villages and towns they passed through. Connie smiled as she remembered her first journey with Will, travelling to Ashton Tracey after their wedding. He'd failed to answer most of *her* questions.

They would stay tonight somewhere between Yeovil and Salisbury, and find an inn near Basingstoke tomorrow night.

If all went well, they should reach London late on Wednesday. It could be a long journey if the girls, or Sukey, did not take to the motion of the coach.

Face that if we come to it, she told herself sternly, and opened her book.

London - Tuesday 11th April

Sir John's butler opened the door to Will's knock, and stood aside to allow him to enter. "I'm afraid Sir John and Lady Tregarth are out for the evening, my lord."

Just as well, Will thought, glancing down at the mud on his boots and breeches, and the rain dripping onto the marble tiles. Sir John's post-chaise had damaged a wheel not long after they'd left Camberley, and he'd hired a horse for the last thirty miles.

"They are expecting you, however, and said they will see you in the morning. Your man, Archer, has been given a room over the stables."

"Thank you, Halley, I'll take the horse round there now."

Stepping back out into the drizzle, Will led the hired gelding around to the mews and into an empty stall. Archer was in the small stable office reading a newspaper, looking quite at home with his feet up on one end of the small desk.

"My lord!" Archer got to his feet, following Will into the stall. "I'll take care of him." He started to unbuckle the saddle girth.

"Lady Wingrave should be here sometime tomorrow," Will said, removing his saddle bags and setting them safely against the wall. "What have you found out?"

"Family arrived at Marstone House on Saturday, my lord. All three young ladies, and a dragon that calls herself a governess."

"Dragon?"

"I talked to Betsy, my lord, maid to the young ladies. That's what she says, acts more like a guard than a governess. She arrived at the Park the day before the young ladies was brought here."

"My father?"

"He was already here, my lord. Been in London a few weeks. There was a great to-do on Monday, when I got here, something about a cancelled dinner. His lordship was in a tearing fury, by all accounts."

"He doesn't know you're in Town?"

Archer shook his head, heaving the saddle off and setting it on a rack. "Not yet, no." He folded the blanket and picked up a brush. "It'll only be a matter of time, though. They won't *want* to tell him, but someone'll tattle—none of the servants like him, but they want to keep their jobs."

Will took another brush from the shelf and started work on the other side of the horse. "Anyone who finds themselves out of work because of this can come to me. Make sure they know that."

"Already said that, my lord."

"Good man, Archer, thank you. You haven't heard anything about marriage contracts being exchanged?"

"No, my lord. And I would have, if it had happened. Seems to be no talk of anything else in the servants' hall."

"What are they saying?"

Archer shrugged. "Bit of a mix. Some say it's a shame the young ladies aren't to have a season, some say they should do what his lordship tells them."

Not all the staff at Marstone House were sympathetic, then. That could make seeing his sisters more difficult. He needed to do that before he tried to talk to his father; if he was still as unreasonable as Miss Glover's report had indicated, he'd do his best to ensure Will did not see his sisters.

"I need to talk to my sisters, Archer, before I call on Lord Marstone formally. Can you arrange that?"

"Might be difficult, my lord. They get locked in at night, haven't been out of the house since they arrived."

Like a damned jail, Will thought savagely. "If only one is possible, I'll see Bella, then. Lady Isabella. But I'd like to see them all if I can." He'd lay money that Bella was the ring-leader, and that note for Harry had been in her handwriting.

"I'll see what I can do, my lord. I'll get one of the footmen to grease some hinges."

"Good idea. See if you can arrange tomorrow night. Have you got enough money?"

"A little more wouldn't come amiss, my lord."

Will emptied his pockets, and handed over his remaining coins. "Just ask if you need more."

"Thank you, my lord. I'll send word when I've got something to report."

CHAPTER 6

ednesday 12th April

Someone must have been watching for them, despite the lateness of the hour. As the coach rolled to a halt in Wimpole Street, the door opened and two footmen carrying flambeaux hurried down the steps. One opened the door of the coach and let down the step before Harry could dismount.

"Etta, we're here now," Connie said, hoping the news would finally make her stop grizzling. She stepped out of the carriage, and lifted Henrietta into her arms.

Lady Tregarth awaited them in the doorway. "Welcome, my dears. Have you had a good...? No, I can see you have not." She turned to the servant standing behind her. "Halley, get Mary to come down, and fetch my sweetmeats box."

Henrietta, her face still flushed from crying, stuck one finger in her mouth and gazed at this new person with wide eyes. Lady Tregarth was elegantly gowned in a red robe à la française, embroidered with a pattern of flowers and birds. "Do you like that?" She held one sleeve towards Henrietta.

"Look, Etta, a pretty bird," Connie said, pointing with her

free hand, grateful for the distraction. Where was Will? She wanted nothing more than to hand Henrietta to someone else—someone who had not had to deal with the girl for two days of travel sickness, boredom and tantrums.

"I don't normally approve of bribes," Lady Tregarth said as the butler returned and handed her a small box. "But it appears Etta has had a trying day."

"As have we all," Connie muttered, taking a piece of sugared orange from the box Lady Tregarth held out. "Here you are, Etta."

By this time Sukey stood in the hallway with a sleeping Sarah in her arms, Kate behind her holding the baby's basket and all the bags of food, toys, and blankets that went with taking small children on a long journey. Another young maidservant was peering at Sarah's face.

"Mary." The young maid came to stand beside Lady Tregarth. "Lady Wingrave, this is Mary, who will be assisting your own maid in the nursery."

"Etta, this is Mary." Connie was relieved to see Mary's wide smile. "Say hello to Mary."

Henrietta shook her head.

"Hello, Etta," Mary said. Glancing at Connie for permission, she reached out and took Henrietta's hand. "Do you want to come upstairs with me? There's a lonely dolly who needs someone to play with."

Henrietta reached out, and Connie thankfully put her down.

"Walk," she demanded, and Mary led her to the foot of the stairs. Connie rubbed her forehead as the pair of them slowly climbed upwards, Sukey following behind with Sarah.

"Thank you for allowing us to stay, my lady," Connie said, turning back to her hostess. "I hope you don't end up regretting it."

"I'm sure I will not. Don't worry, my dear, my two were

just as bad at that age. Will arrived last night, but he is out at the moment." Lady Tregarth's gaze moved beyond Connie's shoulder.

"Lady Tregarth, this is Miss Glover."

"Miss Glover, you will be in the back guest room. It is quite small, I'm afraid, but with Harry here and Lord Wingrave's family, it was all I had left."

Connie warmed to Harry's mother even further—she hadn't been sure what reception Kate would receive. Used to being treated as something between gentry and servant, Kate probably wouldn't have minded a room next to the nursery, but it was an unexpected kindness of Lady Tregarth to treat her as a proper guest.

"Now, tea, wine, or do you wish to go to your room?" Lady Tregarth asked. "Did you dine on the journey?"

"A large glass of wine, please," Connie said. "No food for me, thank you. We ate a couple of hours ago." She glanced at Kate, who shook her head.

In the parlour, Connie sipped wine while Kate told her story to Lady Tregarth, gradually relaxing in a chair that did not rock and sway, to the sound of gentle adult voices.

"Didn't Will tell you all this when he arrived last night?" she asked, when Kate finished.

"Yes, of course. But you can never get the *full* story from a man, my dear. They omit all the really interesting details."

Connie exchanged an amused glance with Kate. She wasn't sure this particular story held any juicy morsels, but she saw Lady Tregarth's point.

"I've never met Marstone," Lady Tregarth said. "But from what Will has said over the years, it seems he is something of a martinet."

"He did stress the necessity of instilling obedience and submission to authority when he employed me, my lady," Kate said, her earnest tone belied by a curl to her lips.

"Which you signally failed to achieve. Tell me, Miss Glover, did you even *try?*" There was no criticism in Lady Tregarth's tone.

"Within reason, yes. There are some matters on which others may have more knowledge of how things should be done, and how the world works. But I would not teach anyone to submit to this kind of marriage arrangement without question."

Lady Tregarth nodded. "And those who have more knowledge are generally those who have been in the world longer and observed with intelligence, not just those of the male sex."

Connie met Kate's eyes, her brows raised. She had not expected quite such a forthright confirmation of her own views.

"Do you not agree, ladies?"

"Well, yes," Connie said. "I was not expecting…" Her voice tailed off—effectively suggesting that her hostess did not have a mind of her own was not the most polite of things to say.

"There are more women who think that way than you perhaps realise, Lady Wingrave." Lady Tregarth ran a hand over her gown. "I am fond of pretty gowns, and dote on my grandchildren, but that does not mean my mind is confined to only those areas."

"I'm sorry if I gave that impression, Lady Tregarth," Connie said.

"Oh, no offence taken, my dear. I will enjoy conversing more on this head, but for now I will leave you to settle in. I have found out a little about Marstone's plans for his daughter, but that should wait until everyone is gathered in the morning." She stood and rang the bell. "Halley will show you to your rooms. Just ask if you need anything. Sleep well, my dears."

~

"One o'clock and all's well!"

Will, shadowed in the entrance to the mews, waited until the watchman turned the corner before creeping along behind Archer to the Marstone House stables. He'd spent the best part of the day at Tattersalls and in various clubs and gaming houses, trying to gather gossip about Lord Drayton, or about his own family. Now, his weariness dropped away as he was about to effectively break in to his father's house.

"They're expecting me?" Will kept his voice low. He checked the keys were still in his pockets—Bella's on the left, the key to the twins' room on the right.

"Betsy said she'd told them," Archer confirmed, his voice just as quiet.

Inside the stables, Will swore under his breath as his foot kicked against something, making a metallic clatter. They froze. A couple of horses whickered quietly, but no-one else stirred. Perhaps Archer had warned the stable hands.

When they reached the garden, a half moon shining through a thin layer of cloud showed the paths as pale strips between the darker flower beds. Their slow steps minimised the crunch of gravel beneath their feet, but that small sound was preferable to the noise they might make if they tripped over a low hedge or became entangled in rose bushes.

Will noted Archer's smile of satisfaction as the back door opened easily to his touch. A faint glow of light ahead came from a lamp at the bottom of the back stairs. Taking a candle from his pocket, Will lit it from the lantern flame, then removed his shoes and left them by the back door. Archer did the same, and the two men mounted to the second floor, treading at the edges of the steps to reduce creaks.

Will cracked open the door between the stairs and the upper corridor, and they listened for a moment. Hearing nothing, he stepped through, leaving Archer waiting at the top of the stairs.

Bella's room was almost opposite, Archer had said. Will first tried the latch but, as he'd expected, the door was locked. The key turned with a quiet snick, and Will slipped inside and locked the door behind him. The girls' new, and very strict, chaperone slept in the room next to Bella's, according to Betsy's information.

"Will?" Bella's question was barely a breath.

"Yes." His candle showed her head peeping out from a gap in her bed curtains, dark hair in a braid beneath a lacy cap. Even in the flickering glow, he could tell the girl he'd last seen three years ago was turning into a woman, her face less rounded. He set the candle on a table near the bed, and went to sit beside her.

"Oh, Will, thank you for coming. I made a real mess of trying to come to you for help." She leaned over and hugged him. "You will save them, won't you?"

He gave her shoulders a squeeze. "I can't promise, Bella, you know that. If the marriage contracts have been signed there's—"

"They haven't. Papa was ranting about ungrateful boys who wanted to inspect the goods before signing." She giggled, her hand over her mouth to muffle the sound. "They were supposed to take Papa's word for it that Theresa and Lizzie would make good wives."

"They? Miss Glover said that Father had come to an arrangement with Lord Drayton for Theresa. Who does he have planned for Lizzie?"

"Oh, Miss Glover. Is she all right, Will? I didn't think she'd lose her job because we ran away. It wasn't her fault."

Marstone probably thought it was—for not reducing the girls' spirits so much that running away would not even occur to them.

"I'll make sure she gets another position," Will promised. "Whose idea was it—Theresa's?" Will was almost certain it wasn't.

Bella shook her head. "She was too busy crying."

"Have some sympathy, Bella! It was her future being bargained away, not yours."

"Not *yet*." Amazing how much feeling could be put into a whisper.

"Let's concentrate on today's problem, shall we?" Will suggested. "Who has Father arranged for Lizzie?"

"A Mr Carterton. It seems very strange to settle for a mere Mister, don't you think?"

"Perhaps he's the heir to a peer? There must be some title in his future, knowing Father. I'll see what I can find out." He'd heard no talk about that connection during today's reconnaissance.

"What are you going to do, Will?"

"I need to know more about them first, Miss Impatience!" He reached out and gently tugged her braid. "Have you seen Lord Drayton yet?"

He heard a muffled snort. "No, none of us have. That's why I've been locked in my room during the day as well as at night."

"What did you—?"

A sound from the doorway reached them, the scraping of a key.

"Miss Furniss!" Bella whispered. "Will, she mustn't find you here!"

Will rolled across the bed, and dropped to the carpet on the side away from the door. It was a tight fit, but he just managed to squeeze under the bed. As he did so, he heard the rustle of bedclothes, and Bella's bare feet came into sight.

"Who's there?" she called.

"I came to check on you, Lady Isabella." A female voice, its tone censorious. "I heard a noise from this room. Why is there a candle lit at this time in the morning?"

"I couldn't sleep," Bella said. "I was reading."

More light flickered—Miss Furniss must be in the room now, looking around.

"It sounded as if you were talking to someone."

"I was talking to myself. Who else do I have to talk to, being locked in here?" Bella's voice rose in indignation. Not entirely feigned, Will thought.

"Well, do not. You will disturb other people."

There was no sound for a good ten seconds, then Bella spoke again. "It seems no-one is stirring, Miss Furniss. I don't think anyone would hear me unless they had their ear pressed against the door."

Will grimaced—this was not the time to antagonise the woman. But there was no response other than moving shadows and a faint rustle. Miss Furniss looking around the room, he guessed, resisting the urge to wriggle further into his hiding place. Thank goodness Marstone's housekeeper was efficient—the last thing he needed now was dust beneath the bed making him sneeze.

"Well, get back into bed, girl. Get to sleep."

Will heard the door close and the key turn.

"That's 'Lady Isabella' to you," Bella muttered. At least she'd had the sense not to say it to the woman's face. More faint sounds—probably Bella going to listen by the door. Then, finally, her feet reappeared beside the bed. "You can come out now, Will."

Will shuffled out. "You do this deception business far too readily, brat." He settled himself on the mattress again. "Was that your new governess?"

"She's our guard, really. She doesn't try to teach us anything." Will heard a sigh in the darkness.

"What did you do to make Father have you locked in?"

41

"I helped curl Theresa's hair. I made the curling iron too hot."

"Good grief!" It showed initiative, if not much sense. "Bella, how much damage did you do?"

"Only a little, but Papa had to cancel a dinner that Lord Drayton was invited to. Theresa still smelled of burned hair."

"Didn't Theresa object to this?"

"No. I did ask her first, honestly! It was two nights ago—after your man told Betsy you were on the way. Now Lord Drayton's gone out of town for a mill, or a cockfight. Something we young ladies are not supposed to know about, anyway. Papa wasn't pleased about that either."

I'll bet he wasn't. "Not showing enough respect for the great Earl of Marstone?"

"Something like that. I stop listening." There was silence for a moment, then her tone was more subdued. "Will, you can save them, can't you?"

"I don't know." He wanted to reassure her, and the other two, but he wouldn't promise something he could not guarantee. "I'll do my best. I'll send word via Betsy, if I can."

"Thank you, Will." She hugged him again. "I wish I could see Lady Wingrave and the babies."

"I think it best if we don't even try, Bella. There's no point in making Father even angrier than he already is." He hesitated, but he may not get the chance to see Bella again for some time. "Bella, Harry Tregarth got a letter that pretended to be from Connie."

The total silence told him he was right—it *had* been Bella's writing. "Bella?" It was difficult having this kind of discussion when he couldn't see her face.

"I'm sorry, Will, it wasn't a nice thing to do, and I was wrong anyway. I told Theresa what I'd done when Papa's steward brought us all back to the Park. She *used* to think she was in love with him, but that was years ago."

"It's a good thing you were caught, Bella. Travelling on the public stage would not have been safe at all."

"So Miss Furniss told me. Several times!"

He chuckled at her indignation. "You need to think things through before jumping into action," he said.

"As you always did?"

"Touché, brat." That was a fair comment. "I'd better go now, I want to have a word with the twins."

"Thank you, Will." She gave him another hug.

He turned the key in the lock, but made no further move for a minute. When it seemed that no-one was about to investigate the noise he'd made he slipped out, locking the door behind him. According to Archer, Theresa and Lizzie shared a room three doors down the corridor on the other side of the door to the servants' stairs—that meant he had to pass Miss Furniss' room.

A floorboard creaked and he paused, ready to make a dash for the stairs, but there was no answering sound behind any of the doors along the corridor. The key to the twins' room turned as easily as Bella's had. Will slipped inside and locked the door.

"Will!" The girls had a lamp between their beds, with the bed curtains drawn back. Will made out Lizzie setting a book down and throwing the covers back before Theresa flung herself against him. "Will, you came!"

"Hush, Theresa!" Will hissed the command. Theresa hadn't raised her voice, but even normal talk might be heard. Lizzie padded over to them, pulling a robe around her, only the glimmer of her smile visible in the dim light.

Theresa put one hand over her mouth, her eyes wide. "Sorry, Will."

"Are you both well?" Will asked, giving Theresa's shoulders a squeeze, then doing the same to Lizzie. It was good to see them again, even if this visit had to be brief.

"Well enough," Theresa said.

Lizzie shrugged. "I thought London would be exciting, but all we've done is visit the mantua maker."

"We're only getting new gowns so Papa can marry us off!"

"Theresa, do you want me to try to prevent this marriage?" Attempting to run away should be a sufficient indication, but it was as well to check.

She nodded. "Please!"

"Me, too," Lizzie whispered. "We want to have a season first, at least, like—"

The floorboard in the corridor creaked again. *Damn.* It must be the dragon—Archer would not have come into the corridor.

"Back to bed," Will whispered. "Go!" He took up a position behind the door. The girls hurried into their beds, pulling the covers up to their chins just as a key turned in the lock. Will stood still, hardly daring to breathe as the door opened. Miss Furniss stepped just far enough into the room for him to see her shape beyond the door.

"What's the matter, Miss Furniss?" Lizzie asked. "Why have you woken us up?"

To Will's irritation, the woman did not move. He couldn't slip out past her, and she was bound to see him if she made the slightest attempt to look around the room.

Does it matter? He'd seen the girls; his father could no longer prevent that.

Yes, it does. Avoiding detection would save many of the servants unpleasant interviews in the morning as Marstone or the butler tried to find out who'd helped him to get in.

"Miss Furniss!" Theresa's voice was far louder now than when she had greeted Will. "*Why* have you disturbed us in the middle of the night?"

"I heard you speak, Ther—"

"*Lady* Theresa, Miss Furniss." Theresa's voice was even louder now, almost a shout. "*Lady* Theresa!"

In spite of the situation, Will grinned in the darkness at this show of spirit. He expected that from Bella; it was good to see Theresa could stand up for herself. But she'd wake others if she spoke so—

"Help! Help!"

Banging sounded from along the corridor, and the cry came again, almost a shriek. Will's heart accelerated. Bella?

Miss Furniss spun around and stepped out. Will made to follow her, but paused when he felt Theresa's hand on his arm.

"Wait a minute." She put her head out of the door as Will let out a breath of relief. Theresa had *expected* Bella to make a noise.

They heard Miss Furniss demanding to know what was wrong, then Theresa turned back to Will. "Now, Will. The dragon's gone into Bella's room."

"Well done, Bella," Will muttered beneath his breath as he dashed across the corridor, Archer opening the door for him when he reached the stairs.

Connie awoke to the sound of the door opening. It was still dark, with only the dim glow of the lamp she'd left burning.

"Will?"

"Yes." He turned up the lamp. "Sorry to wake you."

She sat up in bed as he shrugged himself out of his coat. "You're very late, where have you been?"

His teeth flashed pale in the darkness as he grinned. "Nagging me already, wife?"

"No, just curious. I was hoping you'd be here when we

arrived." He didn't need to hear the details of Henrietta's travel sickness and misbehaviour. Not at the moment.

"I've been to see my sisters."

"At this time of night?"

"Indeed. I'll tell you all about it in the morning." He sat on the bed, one hand reaching out to stroke her hair. "Are you sleepy?"

The usual warmth spread through her at his touch, his obvious intention. "Not any more."

CHAPTER 7

Thursday 13th April

Harry and Kate were already conversing with Will in the breakfast parlour when Connie arrived. Sir John and Lady Tregarth entered a few minutes later, and talk turned to business as soon as Jenkins had laid out the dishes and left the room.

Sir John shook his head as Will described how he'd seen Bella and the twins, and his eyes narrowed when the name Carterton was mentioned.

"Do you know Mr Carterton, Sir John?" Connie asked.

"I know his father," Sir John said. "I think we should concentrate on Drayton first; that agreement seems nearer to being completed. An... acquaintance of mine says Drayton is deep in debt, and speculated that Marstone must be providing a large dowry. Did you find out anything, Wingrave?"

Will nodded. "From what I've gathered in the clubs, Drayton's not the worst marriage prospect in the world, but he's far from the best. He appears to spend his time at sporting events or gaming, mostly losing, and the gossip is that his

47

father has put his foot down and wants him to secure the succession."

"Sounds familiar, eh, Will?" Harry said.

"Harry!" Lady Tregarth hissed. Connie was amused to see a slight flush rise to Harry's cheeks at the reprimand.

"In a way." Will answered as if he'd taken the comment seriously. "However Drayton isn't being forced into it, as far as I can gather, merely taking the path of least resistance. His father also has more justification than mine did. Marstone still has Uncle Jack, whereas if Drayton dies without an heir the marquessate will go to a distant cousin."

"What's he like as a person, though, Will?" Connie asked. "Marstone isn't going to listen to you, so you have to persuade Drayton that the marriage wouldn't suit him. Or at least to not rush into it until Theresa has had time to get to know him."

"A bit of an addlepate, by all accounts," Will said.

"He wouldn't care for an intelligent wife, then?" Lady Tregarth suggested. "One who is interested in politics, or enjoys discussing literature?"

"I doubt it, not from what I heard," Will said.

"Or perhaps one who is extravagant and used to getting her own way?" Connie added, guessing what Lady Tregarth was suggesting.

"Lady Theresa isn't like that, though," Kate put in. "She's intelligent enough, but..." She pressed her lips together, colour rising to her cheeks.

"Please, Miss Glover, just say what you think," Will urged. "Bella was always the most... enterprising of the three of them."

"Theresa is easily led," Kate confirmed. "She's generally happy enough with the usual required accomplishments— embroidery, watercolours. Elizabeth is more bookish, and loves her music. Both have shown little sign of rebellion—

other than trying to escape when they learned they were about to be married to strangers, and we know that was Isabella's idea. Theresa may be content if Lord Drayton leaves her at his country seat—if he has one. But…" She shook her head.

"But she may *not* be content," Connie added. "And 'contentment' is surely not the highest one should aim for?" It was something she would have settled for, before her marriage, but the twins should have a chance at the happiness she had found with Will.

"It is the way of the world," Sir John put in. "Amongst our class, at least."

"So was burning witches, once." Connie bit her lip. "I'm sorry, Sir John, that was rather rude of me."

"I'm playing devil's advocate, my dear," Sir John replied, his smile showing he'd taken no offence.

"I would wish more for my sisters," Will said.

"It doesn't matter what Theresa is like," Lady Tregarth put in. "The important thing is what Drayton *thinks* she is like."

"I've heard he frequents White's," Harry said. "Will, you could congratulate him on picking an intelligent wife with a mind of her own."

"Commiserate, rather," Sir John said.

"Indeed. Or commend him for his tolerance, or some such thing," Connie added. "All this depends on your running across him before any announcement is made, though."

"Connie, I think I should introduce you to my acquaintance in Town," Lady Tregarth said. "If you are happy to leave the children to Miss Glover's supervision, you and I will spend today on morning calls."

"Wouldn't that just confirm the gossip about Drayton?" Will asked. "So far, thankfully, rumours of his impending marriage are just that—it has not yet gone too far to avoid scandal if we can make him change his mind."

"Oh no," Lady Tregarth responded. "*We* will not bring up the subject. But once people work out who Connie is, they will bring it up themselves. We could deny all knowledge, but still say how surprising it is that Drayton should contemplate such a wife, if the stories are true. Word will get to Drayton soon enough." She turned to Kate. "You must tell me all about Bella, Miss Glover. I think she should be our model."

"Does it matter?" Connie asked. "Can you not just invent a personality that Drayton won't like?"

Lady Tregarth shook her head. "Theresa will eventually come into society, and the gossips have long memories. Someone will realise I was inventing a story, and I would rather not get a reputation for spreading untruths."

That was a good point. "So if Bella really is the kind of girl who would challenge Drayton, you could just admit to having described the wrong sister." Connie suppressed a laugh. Lady Tregarth was a natural conspirator, it seemed.

"I'm quite happy to leave that side of things to you ladies," Will said.

"And you and I will try to win money from Drayton at cards, Will," Harry added. "What about this Carterton chap, Papa?"

"Lord Carterton's a baron, has a seat somewhere in Kent, I think," Sir John said. "High Tory."

"A political alliance, then," Will suggested, "if the man's only heir to a barony. We'll see if we can run him down in the clubs." He took a deep breath. "*After* I've tried to see my father."

Lady Tregarth smiled. "If that's all settled, we can relax and enjoy our breakfast."

$\mathcal{I}$t was noon when Will presented himself at the house in Grosvenor Square.

"M..my lord!" The young footman managed to stammer a greeting when he opened the door.

"Ah, Langton. I've come to see my father." Will made no move to enter. If the footman had been ordered not to let him in, it wasn't fair to just push past. Marstone had fired people for less.

The footman swallowed, the bob of his Adam's apple visible in spite of his starched neck cloth. "Um, I have orders not to let you in, my lord."

"Do your orders allow you to summon Mowbray?" The butler, at least, might be secure enough in his position to ask Marstone if Will could be admitted.

Langton left Will standing on the doorstep with the front door ajar. Just as well it's not raining, he thought, leaning against the railings.

Some passers-by paused to stare, turning their eyes away and walking on when Will lifted his hat politely. A movement in one of the ground floor windows caught his eye, but when he peered more closely whoever it was had gone. He suppressed a smile—his father would not like gossip to arise from people seeing Will waiting on the front steps.

Finally the door opened wide. "Would you step inside, my lord?" Mowbray's face was carefully neutral. "His lordship will see you in his study when he is free."

"Thank you, Mowbray. Have some coffee sent to the library, will you?"

The butler's mouth opened, then closed again as he bowed. "Yes, my lord." He stopped to say something to Langton, waiting at the far end of the hall, and the footman took up a position at the bottom of the stairs.

Will shrugged. Marstone had probably given orders to keep him kicking his heels in the hallway, and to prevent him going up to the parlour to see the girls. The library door wasn't far from the foot of the stairs; the footman stiffened as he approached.

"Don't worry, Langton, I'm not going try to get past you."

The footman relaxed visibly. "I'm sorry, my lord, but my orders—"

Will gave the man a friendly nod. "I know."

In the library, he settled himself in a leather-covered chair with a book. He might ask Archer to find out more about Langton. The footman might be a potential ally if he knew Will would take care of his future employment.

His father was looking much older than the last time Will had seen him, with sagging cheeks and bloodshot eyes. He was fatter, too, and from the way he was leaning back in his chair, he must be resting one foot on a stool beneath the desk.

"Well, boy, what have you to say for yourself?" The Earl of Marstone's tone was impatient. It could have been worse,

Will reflected. At least he'd been admitted—and if Bella's diversion last night had raised the household, Marstone wasn't associating him with it.

Will ignored the low armchair set in front of his father's desk. An upright chair stood nearby, suitable for someone working at the desk. Will moved that over, setting it at an angle to give him room to lean back and cross one leg over the other. He'd come here to try to mend matters between them, as far as he could, but not at the expense of accepting Marstone's usual trick of having his subordinates look up to him.

"I just came to see how you are getting on, Father, as I'm in Town with my family."

The earl stared at Will, his brows drawing together. He'd been expecting immediate confrontation, Will guessed.

"Things are doing on well at Ashton Tracey," Will went on, as if the earl would be interested. "The improvements I've made to the farms are beginning to allow an increase in rents." He resisted the temptation to say that Marstone's steward could do with learning from his own experience.

"You've no heir yet," Marstone stated.

"Be fair, Father, I'm trying."

"Two girls. Hmpf. And… what, nearly a year since the last?"

"Ten months," Will said.

"When's the next due? Shouldn't be more than a few months."

"Lady Wingrave is…" Will's words dried up as the implications of his father's words dawned on him. There'd been just over a year between Henrietta's birth and Sarah's. Connie had had no trouble with either confinement, but he'd not liked seeing her so tired after Sarah. He'd vowed to make sure there was a longer gap this time.

His father's attitude wasn't unusual, though, even if Will

disagreed with it. He didn't recall his mother having continuous pregnancies in the years before Theresa and Lizzie had been born, but Marstone already had Alfred to inherit and himself as a spare.

"Not for some time," Will said, frowning as he worked out dates. Theresa and Lizzie, ten years younger than himself, had been born after Uncle Jack left for India. Had the rift between the brothers made Will's father want a third son, to make absolutely sure his brother could not inherit the title? Will's anger rose as vague memories surfaced of his mother being with child again before Bella was born—he'd been at school then, and only learned of it from servants' comments he'd overheard. She must have miscarried that child.

"What are you staring at, boy?"

His father's impatient words pulled Will from his abstraction, and he drew a deep breath. His mother had been unwell for some time after Bella's birth. Had she died as the result of yet another pregnancy after that? If his supposition was correct, his father had caused his mother's death because of his obsession with cutting Jack from the inheritance.

The best revenge is to be unlike him who performed the injury.

He'd followed that advice before, and he was doing it now, as far as begetting an heir went. He'd be sorry, of course, if he never had a son of his own, but he didn't want one at the expense of Connie's health.

"Nothing," Will said. "I'm staring at nothing." Nothing he wanted to be like, nothing he respected.

"Why are you here, Wingrave?" The earl frowned. "Nothing to do with the—?"

"My wife thinks we should be on speaking terms, Father," Will said, not wanting to have to lie outright by denying his interest in the marriage arrangements Marstone was making. "She wished me to call on you, and I have done so."

He stood. His simmering anger would boil over if he

stayed. If cordial relations were ever to be resumed—no, initiated—it would not be today. "I bid you good day, sir."

"Wait, you don't just—"

Will closed the study door behind him, cutting off his father's words. Langton was waiting on the landing to escort him out of the house, the corners of his mouth turning down as Marstone's shouts penetrated the closed door.

"May we walk to the next call?" Connie asked, as she stood with Lady Tregarth on Brooke Street. "I can't face another cup of tea at the moment, or more questions."

"By all means." Lady Tregarth set off, her maid falling in behind them. "Be fair, though, my dear. There was gossip when Will suddenly vanished from society, and although he's been back to Town since, he hasn't been to any social events. You've been a mystery to them."

"What does it matter to—?" Connie shook her head. Gossip *wasn't* the business of the people doing the speculating—that was the point of it. "Do you enjoy these visits?"

"Not much," Lady Tregarth admitted. "I enjoy the theatre or opera more, or just seeing a few good friends. But it helps John if I can keep abreast of any gossip about political figures." Connie heard a chuckle. "Some wives have a lot more influence on their husbands than those men care to admit."

"I suppose Will will be involved in politics when he inherits," Connie said, not relishing the prospect. That would mean spending more time in Town.

"That isn't the only reason," Lady Tregarth went on. "When my grand-daughters are old enough for marriage, the wider my social circle, the better their chances of making a match that suits them. The boys, too."

"How old are they?" Connie asked. "They must be quite young if you keep the nursery here furnished for them."

"Jane, the oldest, is ten," Lady Tregarth said. "But the younger ones still enjoy playing, and I suspect Susannah is with child again." She sighed. "I wish Harry would find a wife —Will seems to be thriving now he's left his bachelor ways behind him."

Connie blushed. "I think so," she said, almost too quietly to be heard. "Do you wish Harry to marry a titled lady?"

Lady Tregarth stopped, and Connie turned to look at her, afraid her question had been impertinent.

"Why do you ask that?"

"I'm sorry, it's not my—"

"Good heavens, after all the questions I've let you be subject to today, that's nothing. No, I wondered if you had a particular reason for your…" Her brows drew together, then a smile spread across her face.

"Miss Glover—it must be. She's the only person both you and Harry know. Unless there's someone in Devonshire?"

"No, my lady. This is pure speculation on my part. I like Kate, very much, and I like Harry too. I think they would suit, once Harry stops…" She didn't want to criticise her hostess' son.

"Once Harry stops baiting Will about your marriage and grows up." Lady Tregarth was still smiling.

"Do you approve?"

"It's not up to me to approve or not, it will be Harry's choice," Lady Tregarth said. "But I think that could be a good match. I'd much rather he married someone like Kate than a titled ninny, or some miss straight from the schoolroom who would bore him witless within a month." She walked on. "Now you have suggested that possibility, I wonder if I could help Miss Glover find a position in London."

"But—"

"Don't worry, my dear, I will not meddle beyond giving them a chance to meet now and then. Now, our next call is to Lady Margate, who I understand is a confidante of Drayton's mother. She is our best prospect for having our story repeated in the right ears. The marchioness rules the roost at home, I gather, and I suspect she won't be any more delighted than her son at the prospect of an intelligent bride with ideas of her own."

riday 14th April

"That's him," Harry said. "Far corner, reading a newspaper. Racing results, I expect."

At last. After spending most of yesterday looking for Drayton—subtly—they had finally learned he was not expected back in Town until late that night. Will had given up and gone home, relieved that Connie and Lady Tregarth had made more progress than he had. It was now early evening and Will had been on the point of giving up again when Harry spotted their quarry.

The morning room in White's was thin of company, and Will had a clear view of Lord Drayton. His clothing was nothing out of the ordinary—if he was the spendthrift rumour suggested, he was not wasting money on his clothing. He was not fat, precisely, although his stomach strained at the buttons of his waistcoat and his face looked a little puffy. He had a large glass of claret in front of him, and a folded newspaper that he was studying with furrowed brow.

"Do we just walk up and introduce ourselves?" Will was reluctant to do so; he wanted the encounter to appear casual.

"Wait a moment," Harry said. "Let's see who else is here."

Will followed him through the rooms until Harry paused in the doorway to the coffee room. "Ah, Freddy Rodbourne. You won't know him—his father's a friend of my father."

"Will he know Drayton?" Will kept his voice low.

"Let's see, shall we?" Freddy bore a certain resemblance to Lord Drayton—running a little to fat, with puffy eyes that suggested too many late nights.

"Rodbourne, well met!" Harry's tone was artificially jovial to Will's ears, but Rodbourne didn't appear to find anything wrong with it.

"Tregarth, fancy seeing you here." He put his newspaper aside.

"This is Wingrave." Harry tilted his head towards Will. "We're in search of a game."

"Why not?" Rodbourne's face became more animated. "Hazard?"

"Whist, if we can find a fourth," Harry said. "Saw someone in the morning room who might do. Drayton, I think, although I've never been introduced."

"Oh, I know Algy," Rodbourne said, pushing his chair back and getting to his feet. "C'mon, I'll do the honours."

Ten minutes later the four men had taken a table in the card room, and Harry was dealing. He and Will had taken opposite seats without the formality of cutting for partners, but neither of the other men seemed to mind.

"How about a guinea a game to start with?" Will asked. "And ten on the rubber?" Not daring stakes, by any means, but better to test the skill of their opponents before risking too much money. He hadn't put his efforts into improving the land and revenues at Ashton Tracey to throw it away now.

Drayton shrugged. "The night is young, we can make it

more interesting later." He sorted his cards and played a queen, then raised a hand to summon a nearby waiter.

"My lord?"

Drayton tapped his glass. "Claret. Keep 'em filled."

Excellent—now all Will and Harry had to do was to prevent Drayton noticing that their glasses were not being topped up at the same rate.

Rodbourne and Drayton won the first rubber by three games to two, with the aid of some carefully chosen poor cards from Will and Harry. Other men came and went in the gaming room, casting cursory glances at the players before finding their own games. Will exchanged a nod with Harry as Rodbourne dealt the next hand; things were proceeding according to plan. They would try to win the next rubber, then lose a couple more.

"I hear rumours that we're about to be related," Will ventured, as Drayton took the next trick.

"Mm. M'father's sorting it out. Need a bit of help with my debts." He selected a card and played, to the accompaniment of a 'tut' from his partner.

"Brave man," Will said, wasting a high card from his hand. He didn't want Drayton to realise yet that he was outclassed.

"Any man's brave who willingly steps into the parson's mousetrap," Rodbourne said.

"You haven't met Wingrave's sister," Harry put in. "Your trick again, Drayton."

"Sho… So it is. Fancy raising the stakes?" Drayton drained his glass and gestured for the waiter to refill it.

"Not yet." Rodbourne scowled as his partner took another gulp of wine.

"Oh, well. Play on anyway, eh?" Drayton led with a low trump. "What's this about your sister, then, Wingrave?"

"Mind of her own," Will said. "Bit of a crusader as well. You'll get no peace once you come into the title."

"Heh," Harry sniggered. "She'll be writing your speeches for you."

"S'alright, I can't be bothered with that. Let someone else run the country."

"That's what you think," Will muttered. He felt a presence behind him. Turning to tell the waiter to stop hovering, he saw instead another member of the club leaning on the wall watching their game. The man was beyond the pool of light cast by the chandelier; Will got only the impression of sober dress and a slim build, a glass of wine in one hand.

An hour later, Rodbourne played the fourth card of a trick, and Will added the cards to the pile by his elbow. The last trick would be a formality—he'd won again.

"Damme, Wingrave, you have the luck of the devil." Drayton's face was flushed, his words well slurred. He gestured to a waiter to refill his glass. "You, too, Tregarth."

Will laid the seven of hearts on the table. Drayton peered at it then at the card in his hand.

"Play on, Drayton, for God's sake" his partner said. "You've only got one card, and it won't win!"

Drayton laid a two of hearts, the other two discarded clubs and spades. Will collected the trick, and totted up the markers. "Another hundred guineas," he said.

Rodbourne swore and scribbled an IOU, handing it to Tregarth. "I'm off. I don't mind losing money through my *own* lack of skill." If looks could kill, Drayton would be dead on the floor.

"D'you want to play something else, Drayton?" Will asked. "Pity Rodbourne's gone. No bottom, some people."

"I'll make a fourth, if you have no objection?" The shadowed figure pushed himself away from the wall. He was much younger than Drayton, possibly even younger than Will and Harry, with dark blond hair neatly tied back and a pleasant, open face. He seemed to take their acquiescence for granted, sitting in the chair Rodbourne had just vacated and setting his full glass on the table.

"By all means." The man had been watching them, off and on, for some time—if he hadn't realised Drayton was well into his cups he deserved to lose. "Wingrave, Tregarth, Drayton." Will pointed as he spoke.

"Carterton," the newcomer said. "Whose deal?"

Will's hands froze for a moment as he shuffled, then pushed the pack towards Drayton. It was surely too much of a coincidence that both his sisters' prospective suitors now sat at this table. Could Carterton be here as an ally of Drayton?

"Time for better luck," Drayton muttered. "Glad Rodbourne's gone—no skill." He shook his head sadly as he dealt, almost sending the cards off the edge of the table.

"Heard you're getting wed, Drayton," Carterton said, winning the second trick by wastefully trumping his partner's ace of spades. "Better choose one who doesn't talk at the breakfast table. My mother…" He shook his head sadly, laying down an eight of spades to start the next trick.

Harry opened his mouth to object, but Will stopped him with a glare. If Drayton hadn't noticed that Carterton had revoked in the last hand, he wasn't going to tell him.

"Meeting the gal tomorrow night," Drayton said, staring owlishly at the cards in his hand. "Dinner at Marsh… Marshtone House. Get the contracts sorted after that, as long as she's not swivel-eyed or—"

Will cleared his throat loudly.

"Shorry, Wingave. Your sister an' all that."

"Come on, Drayton. Play or give up," Carterton said. "I didn't join in to listen to you bemoaning your sorry fate."

That could be taken as an insult to Theresa, but Will chose not to react. There was something strange going on here. He kept a close eye on Carterton's cards as they played on, the increasingly stuffy air in the card room making his head ache. It was nearly three years since he'd gambled the nights away in clubs like this, and he was no longer used to it.

Carterton's behaviour was inexplicable. He'd hardly touched his wine, and his face and words showed no signs of inebriation. Will had even caught a wry quirk to his lips when he laid a particularly bad choice of card. If this man insisted on marrying Lizzie, sight unseen, Will would have a hard task thwarting him.

Drayton, on the other hand…

Will snapped a card down, and collected the trick. His aim was no longer to give Theresa time to get to know Drayton. He'd already decided on her behalf—that drunken blockhead wouldn't make any woman a decent husband. His goal now was to make either Drayton or Marstone withdraw from any agreement they'd reached.

"Thash me finished," Drayton said at last, eyeing the pile of markers in front of Will. "I'll have to… to ask you to give me shome time to pay up."

"Sorry, Drayton, I'll be leaving Town in a few days," Will said. "Can't hang around. I'm sure you can find the money somewhere."

"You'll give us a chance to win it back, Wingrave, Tregarth?" Carterton asked. "Tomorrow, say?"

"Can't." Drayton shook his head. "Got to go to dinner."

"Dig yourself out of bed by noon," Carterton suggested. "Plenty of time for a few hours' play before then."

Will didn't speak. Carterton was up to something—he didn't know what, but so far his actions had only helped Will's plan. He couldn't believe Drayton would play much better when sober, and winning more money off him would not go amiss. He looked around, raising a hand as a waiter walked into the room with a tray of decanters. "Summon a hackney for Lord Drayton."

The waiter bowed and hurried out again.

"Thash very good of you," Drayton said. "I'll be here."

"This way, my lord." The waiter helped Drayton to his feet, and guided him out through the correct door.

CHAPTER 10

*C*arterton got to his feet. "Shall we retire to the coffee room, gentlemen?"

"What the hell's going on, Will?" Harry murmured as they followed the younger man out.

Will shrugged. He ordered coffee, and gratefully took a deep breath of the clearer air in the coffee room. It was quieter here, too, with men talking quietly in small groups, or sitting with newspapers and decanters of port. Carterton led the way to a table near one of the windows, well away from other members.

"I take it you have no objection to tomorrow's game," Carterton said as they sat down.

Will shook his head.

"I'm hoping you will return my own vowels," Carterton went on. "I can't afford to lose even half the amount I've lost this evening."

"Why would I do that?" Will asked, not denying the request but wanting to hear Carterton's reasons. The man didn't seem particularly anxious about his agreement, which was odd if his losses really were excessive.

"For helping you to increase Drayton's debt to you," Carterton said. "I'm not yet sure how you plan to use that to dissuade him from marrying Lady Theresa, but I'm interested to find out." He broke off as a waiter set a pot of coffee and three cups on the table.

"You seem more certain of Drayton's marriage prospects than anyone else I've spoken to in the last few days," Will said. "What makes you think I'm trying to stop the match? It would be advantageous, I'm sure, to have a future marquess in the family."

"Even a drunken sot like Drayton?" Carterton raised one brow.

Will couldn't argue against that. "From what I heard, Marstone has you lined up to marry Lizzie. If I'm against Theresa's match, why would I help your own prospects by cancelling what you owe me?"

Carterton relaxed back in his seat, giving Will the uneasy feeling that he was no longer in control of the situation.

"You are labouring under a number of misapprehensions, Wingrave, as are our respective parents."

"*Are* you intending to marry Lady Elizabeth?" Harry asked. Will was irritated to see that his friend seemed more amused than anything else.

"My father is a political ally of Marstone," Carterton said to Will, ignoring Harry's question.

"I surmised as much," Will said. "However any political alliance will end the moment I inherit the earldom."

"I'm pleased to hear it." Carterton smiled.

Will's eyes narrowed. "You do not follow your father's political inclinations, then."

"No more than you do yours. Unlike you, however, I am on good terms with my father and he doesn't realise that I don't agree with him." He poured the coffee, and pushed cream and sugar across the table towards Will. "I agreed only to consider the match, despite what your father may have told your sisters."

"Have you spoken to Lizzie?" When he'd seen Bella two nights ago, neither of the prospective spouses had visited.

Carterton smiled, almost a grin. "I dined at Marstone House last night. I have to say that neither Lady Theresa nor Lady Elizabeth sounded like the sister you were describing earlier. They barely said a word, but that was hardly surprising given the way your father glowered at them."

"So what makes you think I'm trying to dissuade Drayton?" Will was beginning to suspect the answer.

"I also made the acquaintance of Lady Isabella. She was not at dinner, but she... accosted me on the way out."

Will rubbed his forehead. *That sounds like Bella!* He could imagine her lurking in a doorway waiting to drag the unsuspecting Carterton into an ante-room.

"In short, Wingrave, I've no intention of marrying a girl straight from the schoolroom who hasn't been in society. Not for any shortcomings in Lady Elizabeth herself, but she should have a chance to meet more people before being legshackled."

Will nodded—that was a sentiment he completely agreed with.

"Marstone is as yet unaware of my decision," Carterton went on. "The occasion to tell him did not arise at dinner, and Lady Isabella's... revelations decided me to keep my counsel for the moment."

Will's lips twitched. He wondered just how direct Bella's revelations had been.

"I am invited to dinner again tomorrow night," Carterton continued. "Drayton should also be present, and I suspect Marstone will be putting him under pressure to sign the marriage contracts. I am willing to help you deter Drayton, if you need my assistance."

"Why?"

"Call it general benevolence," Carterton, regarding Will with a slight tilt of his head. "I'd not see a sister of mine wed to someone like Drayton."

Will gazed at Carterton, who met his eyes squarely. He didn't quite believe in general benevolence, but he couldn't think of any reason not to trust the man, and help from this unexpected source could be very useful.

"I hadn't got as far as working out how to use Drayton's debt to my advantage," he admitted. "I was hoping the idea of an intelligent and outspoken wife might make him think twice."

"That wouldn't work on every man," Carterton pointed out. "Admittedly, it wouldn't take much of a brain to outwit Drayton, but in any case his debts are too great to allow him to turn down a hefty dowry. You may wait some time for him to settle his debt."

"Would your father be annoyed that Drayton's lost money to *you*, Will?" Harry asked.

That's an excellent question.

"Carterton, I'll be grateful for your assistance," Will said. "And if you're willing to lose again tomorrow, the bigger his debt the better." He smiled. "One day we must play when we're both trying to win!"

Carterton nodded and stood. "Until tomorrow, then."

"Time for me to go, too," Will said, when Carterton had left. He suppressed a yawn. "I've no stamina for this kind of thing any more. I'll see you in the morning, Harry."

Spending his evenings with Connie was far more entertaining.

Connie was reading in bed when he returned to the

Tregarths' house in Wimpole Street. She put her book to one side.

"Did you find him?"

"We did indeed." Will described the card game as he undressed, and climbed into bed beside her. She was wearing one of her lacy chemises, and his hand reached for the ribbons at her neck.

She pushed his hand away. "Tell me the rest, Will. What are you planning on doing now Drayton owes you so much money?"

He sighed. "Something Harry said gave me an idea. My father won't care too much that Drayton wastes Theresa's dowry; he *will* mind if Drayton is going to expect help with his future debts as well. My idea is that he asks my father for an increase in Theresa's dowry to pay this new debt of honour."

"The dowry is going to be mostly spent paying off Drayton's debts in any case, isn't it? Will a little more make any difference?" Her gaze became intent, her brows drawing together. "Will, you're not going to duel with Drayton, are you?"

"No, Connie. The threat of it might—"

"No, Will." She knelt up on the bed so she could look him directly in the face. "You could end up being dragged into it anyway, unless you're going to risk being branded a coward."

Will made an effort to keep his gaze on her eyes, not on what the gaping neck of her chemise was revealing. She did have a point. "All right. Not even a threat. But I doubt it will come to that, Connie. The point is that Drayton lost it *to me*. By subsidising Drayton, Marstone will effectively be giving money to me. Ideally, Drayton will also make it clear that he's going to try to win the money back from me."

"Your father will realise he has little chance, even if Drayton does not."

"Indeed."

"How are you going to prime Drayton to say all that convincingly enough? And without him realising you're manipulating him?"

"*I* won't be prompting him. Carterton is invited to the same dinner tomorrow night."

She nodded, sitting back against the pillows. "That could work. Do you trust Carterton?"

"I think so, yes." He put his hand back on the ribbons at her neck and pulled gently. This time she didn't push him away.

Saturday 15th April

Will sipped his ale as he waited for Carterton in a tavern a few streets away from White's. He'd separated the stack of vowels from this afternoon's gaming and last night's. Drayton's IOUs added up to several thousand pounds. He felt a pang of guilt, quickly quashed; Drayton was a fool.

"What an idiot." Carterton spoke as he sat down opposite Will. "He's a poor enough player when he's sober, but to play drunk, and to carry on when he's losing heavily?" He shook his head.

That was how whole fortunes changed hands, Will reflected. Even in his rebellious days, he'd never been that stupid. He pushed Carterton's IOUs across the table.

Carterton took them with a nod of thanks and tucked them into a pocket. "What do you intend to do with that?" He indicated the papers still in front of Will, weighed down by his card case.

"I have an idea. It's not guaranteed to work, but it stands a better chance with your assistance."

"That depends on what you want me to do." Carterton

gazed into his ale for a moment, then back at Will. "Fleecing Drayton doesn't feel right to me. We *were* cheating, in effect."

Will pushed Drayton's vowels towards Carterton. "You can lose the money to him again, if it makes you feel better." That would salve the minor complaints of his own conscience as well. He wondered if Carterton would see the flaw in this plan.

Carterton pushed them back. "I'll need the cash—unless you can think of a plausible reason for how I might have won these from you and then manage to play poorly enough to lose them again to Drayton."

Will nodded. It was almost a pity this man had declined to marry Lizzie; unlike Drayton, he would be an asset to the family. "I'll arrange it," he said. "You are aware, I think, that I am estranged from my father."

Carterton nodded. "Most of society is aware, I'm afraid."

Will explained the idea he'd discussed with Connie the night before. Carterton digested the plan for a moment, then shook his head.

"Do you think it won't work?" Will asked.

"Oh, I think it stands a good chance of working. That was more a comment on your devious— " Carterton cleared his throat. "And an even better chance if Drayton doesn't realise he's being manipulated, which is where I come in, I suppose." Carterton took a mouthful of ale. "Do warn me, Wingrave, if I am ever on the point of getting on the wrong side of you."

Will chuckled. "You've got enough wits to know what you're doing."

"I must inform Marstone soon that I am not going to fall in with his plans. I would prefer to inform my father first, though, which means I will not speak to Marstone about it for a couple of days. I'll put him off if he raises the subject this evening. Do you wish to meet your sisters?"

"If possible, but I can't do that at Marstone House."

"I will insist that I take Lady Elizabeth for a drive in the Park tomorrow," Carterton said. "I'll send word of the time. I'll do my best to bring Lady Theresa along as well." He smiled, but without humour. "You'll need to bring along someone, or something, to distract their chaperone if you wish for a private word."

"Thank you, Carterton. I will be in your debt."

Carterton stood. "I'll remember that. Now I need to extract Drayton from the alehouse where I left him. Your plan won't work if he's too fuddled to get his lines right."

CHAPTER 11

*S*unday *16th April*

Lady Tregarth had borrowed an open carriage for the afternoon. Connie took Will's hand as he helped her in, and she sat next to Lady Tregarth facing forwards. Kate, posing as Lady Tregarth's companion for the afternoon, sat on the backward-facing seat with Henrietta beside her.

Connie smiled as Will and Harry mounted their horses and they all set off. Will had decided that the more distractions there were, the better, if he was to have a private word with his sisters. However three women, an extra man and a toddler seemed excessive to divert the attention of just one chaperone.

The afternoon was cloudy but, unlike the last couple of days, it did not feel like rain. That allowed Will to take all of them with him, but as they turned through the park gates Connie realised it could also pose a problem. The roads through the park were crowded with vehicles, riders and pedestrians; it would not be easy for Will to spot the Carterton carriage.

Lady Tregarth's coachman tooled the horses along at a

sedate pace as Will and Harry rode on ahead. Both wearing dark jackets, they were almost indistinguishable from a distance.

Lady Tregarth waved to a few acquaintances, some of whom Connie recognised from her calls, but did not stop. Henrietta stared wide-eyed at her surroundings, one finger in her mouth; there must be more people here than she'd seen in one place before.

They had completed one circuit, and were about to start another when Harry came cantering over.

"Have you found them, Harry?" Connie asked.

"Yes, a couple of hundred yards ahead, going the same way." Harry pointed with his whip. "It's a black carriage with red seats. I'll ride on and greet Carterton, that shouldn't worry the dragon. Will's waiting further on. Are you ready, Mama?"

"As ready as I'll ever be, Harry," Lady Tregarth said. "Lead on."

Harry said a few words to the coachman and trotted off. Their vehicle put on speed, and it wasn't long before they pulled up beside an open carriage with two young ladies and a gentleman sitting inside, accompanied by an older woman dressed in severe black. Harry was already talking to Carterton. The girl with the brown curls had her eyes on the floor of the coach, her cheeks flushed. Theresa, Connie guessed, feeling embarrassed after Bella's stratagem to have her meet Harry. The blonde girl, looking at Kate, opened her mouth to speak, but Kate stopped her with a small shake of the head.

"Why, Harry, fancy meeting you here," Lady Tregarth said. "And Mr Carterton, too. How nice to see you again."

Connie shouldn't be surprised at Lady Tregarth's aptitude for deception, not after the day they'd spent together on social calls.

"Lady Tregarth." Carterton bowed his head, taking his

cue. Connie had considered the introductions the weak point in Will's plan; there had been no time to let Carterton or the girls know that Lady Tregarth would be addressing them all as if she knew them well.

"And Theresa and Lizzie, how are you, my dears? It's a pleasure to see you in Town. It's about time your father introduced you into society."

Theresa and Lizzie exchanged puzzled glances, but said nothing. Luckily their chaperone's attention was on Lady Tregarth. "My lady, they are not—"

"Why don't I take you for a turn in my carriage?" Lady Tregarth went on, not even looking at the companion. "We can have a comfortable chat. I'm sure your father would have no objection. Kate, dear, get down. I know Mr Carterton will be happy to drive you around for a while. You will be perfectly fine with Miss..." Lady Tregarth looked directly at the chaperone for the first time. Connie bit her lips at Lady Tregarth's imperious manner, envying her aplomb.

"Miss Furniss, my lady. But the young ladies—"

"An excellent idea." This time Carterton spoke over the chaperone's objection. "Do not worry, Miss Furniss, we will keep them in sight." He descended and helped the girls down, then handed Kate in. "Drive on, Bateman."

"But I must keep the girls..." The chaperone's voice faded as Carterton's carriage drew away.

"Lady Tregarth, why do you want to drive with us?" the brown-haired girl asked, eyeing Connie as she spoke with a puzzled frown.

"Will wanted to see you, my dear. He'll be along in a moment. Which one are you?"

"I'm Theresa." She blushed as she looked at Harry, waiting beside the carriage. "I suppose it's all right." Connie took Henrietta onto her lap to make space as the two girls climbed in. Both regarded Connie with curiosity plain on their faces.

"This is Lady Wingrave, your sister-in-law," Lady Tregarth said.

"And this is Henrietta," Connie added. "Etta, say hello to your Aunt Theresa and Aunt Lizzie."

"Oh, we've so wanted to meet you! You look so different from when we saw you in the church!"

"What a darling child—can I hold her?"

"I don't feel old enough to be an aunt."

Approaching the carriage, Will could see his sisters talking with Connie, although the focus of their attention seemed to be Henrietta. Connie was smiling; happy to meet new members of her family, he guessed.

Damn Father.

Connie's childhood had been quite isolated, with only Martha Fancott as a real friend since her sisters had married. He wasn't sure how close she'd been to them, either. Here, she had two girls—women—who could have been good friends from the beginning of their marriage. The girls, too, would have benefitted from being with a sensible woman like Connie and seeing what a marriage *could* be like.

"Will!"

Lizzie's excited squeak diverted him from his thoughts. He fell in beside the carriage as Harry rode off ahead. From a distance, Miss Furniss might not notice who was now talking to the occupants of Lady Tregarth's carriage.

"Lizzie. Hello Teresa."

"Will, did you arrange all this?"

"With help, yes. I wanted to see you properly, without having to whisper in your bedrooms!"

Theresa beamed at him. "Oh, Will, I'm not to marry Lord Drayton after all!"

"What happened?" Carterton's note had only given

the time to meet in the park. Beyond the girls, Connie and Lady Tregarth were listening with unashamed interest.

"Bella said—"

"Bella?"

Theresa nodded. "Papa sent us to our rooms after dinner, when Lord Drayton said he wanted a private interview. Papa was looking pleased, and I thought they were going to sign the contracts."

"But Bella went and listened outside the door," Lizzie said.

"Mowbray was in his pantry," Theresa added. "One of the footmen saw her, but he didn't say anything."

"Bella said he was listening as well."

"But what *happened*?" Will asked. "What did Bella hear?"

"Lord Drayton asked for more money. She couldn't make out what Papa said, then Drayton said it was all right, the money would stay in the family. Then Papa flew into a rage." Theresa's happy smile was gone now.

Lizzie took over. "He was calling you all sorts of names, according to Bella. She didn't understand all of them. And calling Lord Drayton names too, for even talking to you. He said Drayton would get no more money out of him if it would end up in your pockets, and told Drayton he was never to speak to you again."

"We were listening on the landing," Theresa said. "We could hear some of it right up there. Drayton stormed out, shouting he wouldn't be ordered around like that, and he'd find someone else to marry. He didn't want a wife with her nose always in a book anyway."

Drayton had a spine somewhere, then.

"But Theresa doesn't like reading very much, Will. Why would Drayton say that?"

"I'll tell you some other time," Will said.

"Will, Papa will be furious if he finds out that you've talked to us."

"Don't worry about that, my dears," Lady Tregarth said. "At this moment, Miss Glover is telling Miss Furniss how she lost her job, even though she knew nothing about Bella's plan to run away. I think she might decide not to tell your father, even if she realises this is Will, and not still Harry."

"Is Miss Glover going to get another position, Will?" Lizzie asked. "We didn't know Papa would send her away."

"We will make sure she does," Connie put in. "Will, do you think they've been away from their chaperone too long? The longer you're with them, the more chance there is of someone seeing you and word getting to your father."

Will sighed. She was right—and the earl would blame the girls as much as him or Miss Furniss, and had the ability to punish them. Lady Tregarth waved, and Will saw Harry riding back towards them.

"Lizzie, Theresa, I'll try to work out a way of getting my letters to you. Remember one thing, though. Any of the servants who help you are likely to lose their jobs if they are found out, but they will always have a job with me at Ashton Tracey. Lizzie, did Mr Carterton explain—?"

"Yes, Will. I think he wouldn't have been so bad as a husband." She didn't look sorry about it, though.

"I'll try to see you again," he promised, and rode off.

CHAPTER 12

"That seemed to have worked well," Connie said, back in the parlour in Wimpole Street. Will's sisters—her sisters, now—were lovely girls; such a shame that she wouldn't be able to see them again. Was there any way to mend the breach between Will and his father?

"Indeed," Will said, although he didn't look very pleased. Something was still on his mind.

He looked at Lady Tregarth. "Thank you for your help, my lady. I could not have talked to my sisters without you."

"A pleasure, Will. But if you can get word to your sisters, let them know that any servants who need your assistance should come to me. It's a long way to Ashton Tracey. If I can't find them a position here in London, I can at least let them have the fare for the stage."

"Thank you, Lady Tregarth, that is an excellent thought."

"Will, what is wrong?" Connie asked. His expression had not changed—something else must be worrying him.

"It's not over, is it? Father will just set up another arrangement, and possibly with men even less suitable. And Connie, you should be able to enjoy the company of my sisters, but even if Father allowed it, Devonshire is a long journey from here."

"It's just as well you don't live in Northumberland then," Lady Tregarth said, standing up. "I'll leave you two to discuss matters in private, but bear two things in mind. First, you are welcome to stay here as long as you wish, and second, I would enjoy having someone new to introduce to the *ton*."

"What did she mean, Will?" Connie asked as the door closed behind Lady Tregarth. She couldn't be volunteering to take Theresa and Lizzie about, could she? She didn't even know them.

No. Lady Tregarth had meant *her*.

"Connie, I did try to mend things with Father when I saw him on Thursday, but the man's impossible. All I can do is to threaten to disrupt any other marriage he arranges unless I'm sure the girls are happy with it, and that means they need to have been in society."

"Lord Marstone wouldn't expect... wouldn't *let* me take them about, would he?"

"No." Will shook his head. "He'll get one of my aunts to do it. But if I'm to make sure they have a fair chance, I'll need to be here."

Of course. "And you can keep track of what is going on better if I'm here too." The thought of spending the season in Town didn't fill her with dread as it had three years ago. Lady Tregarth would help her, and she'd met several friendly women during their day of social calls.

"Will, can we afford to be in Town for a whole season while the twins are presented?" She'd need enough new gowns to be reasonably fashionable. "And can you be away from Ashton Tracey for several months?"

"Archer and Roberts between them can manage our business there," Will said. "Short of anything really out of the ordinary, that is, and I could go down for a few days every month or so if necessary. It wouldn't be until next year—it's too late to organise everything for them to be presented properly this year. I'll have a word with Talbot, too. He was hinting at wanting someone in Town he could trust as well."

He moved to sit on the sofa beside her and took her hand. "Connie, I know you didn't want to face the *ton* when we first married."

She gave his hand a squeeze. "I've changed since then, Will. Spending the season here isn't something I would choose to do for its own sake, but I will manage. I will enjoy knowing your sisters better." She thought back over the conversation in the Park, and chuckled. "Particularly Bella."

"Ha, yes. She'll be a handful when she's old enough to come out." The amusement quickly faded. "Connie, I need to see my father again. We can go home then, if you wish. Harry and Lady Tregarth will let me know immediately if I need to come back, and Archer has arranged for a couple of the staff at Marstone House to pass on information as well."

They had only arrived four days before. Connie wasn't keen on spending several days in a coach with Henrietta and Sarah again quite so soon. Besides that, it might be better if Will stayed in Town for a week or two, to make sure his father didn't do anything drastic in a fit of revenge.

"Will, how *can* you suggest we go back before I've seen St Paul's, and Westminster Abbey, and the Tower? Then there's the British Museum, and—"

"Enough, wife!" Will leaned over and kissed her cheek. "I'll see Father tomorrow, whether he likes it or not, then I'm at your command."

Monday 17th April

Will had no trouble getting into Marstone House this time.

81

"Mowbray, has Mr Carterton called this morning?"

The butler met his eyes. "Yes, my lord." He cleared his throat.

Will waited.

"His lordship was most unhappy with the outcome of the visit," the butler finally said.

That was useful to know. "Thank you, Mowbray."

"His lordship is in his study, my lord."

The earl was sitting in his usual place behind the desk, eyes narrowed and lips compressed. Will sat as he had before, and waited for his father to speak.

"I have you to thank for the collapse of a very prestigious marriage arrangement, I suppose," Marstone said at last.

"Oh, did Drayton change his mind?" It wouldn't do for the earl to guess that he already knew. "That's a pity, I was looking forward to many more lucrative gambling sessions with him."

"You cheated him!"

Will suppressed his irritation at the accusation. That was his father's anger talking, spite at being thwarted. "Be careful with your accusations, Father. It would do the family name no good for my honour to be called into question."

"Your *honour*? You spend your days gambling, whoring—"

"No, Father." Will spoke more forcefully this time. "Unlike some men, I've kept my marriage vows. And the only gambling I've done since my marriage is with Drayton."

The earl glared at him. "Do you mean you went looking for Drayton?"

"Yes, I did. With the sole purpose of winning money from him. There's really no need to cheat when playing against a drunken fool. Is that really the kind of blood you want in the next generation of this family?"

"The man will be a marquess."

"Indeed, and looking set to gamble away his entire

fortune. Thankfully, it seems now that his marchioness will *not* be one of my sisters." He had to remember he wasn't supposed to know any of the details his sisters had passed on. "Besides, you must have disapproved of his gambling, or why have the marriage arrangements been called off? *I* did not tell him to change his mind."

"He is a damned fool. He wanted—" The earl took a deep breath as his face darkened. "That is none of your business."

"Oh, it is," Will countered. "My sisters deserve to have a proper season before they marry. *All* of them. If you arrange another marriage for any of them before that happens, I will thwart it. Carterton didn't come up to scratch either, did he?"

"Carterton? You meddled there, too?" The earl's face was red now, his breathing hard. Will wondered if he was about to have an apoplexy.

Would the earl calm down if he knew that Will hadn't needed to intervene there? He shrugged. Let him think what he wanted to.

"Theresa and Lizzie will have a season next year, Father. Aunt Honora or Aunt Aurelia can see to it—I'm sure you can persuade one of them. At that point you may start to think about their marriages."

"What makes you think you can tell me—?"

"What makes *you* think I cannot counter your plans? Your attempt to hold the sale of Ashton Tracey over my head failed, didn't it?" He stood. There was no point continuing this argument. "I have more influence than you like to think, Father, and I *will* protect my sisters."

He left while the earl was still gasping for words.

Will leaned on the railing, gazing down at the floor of St Paul's cathedral a hundred feet below. Above him, spring sunshine poured through the windows above the gallery and made patterns of light on the opposite wall.

Connie was further on around the gallery. They'd already had a tour of the ground floor of Wren's masterpiece and by the time they'd climbed up here, Will had learned more about the place than he'd ever wanted to know.

But he was content standing here with only a quiet murmur of voices from visitors below them, and the distant voice of the verger talking about inner and outer domes, brick cones and stone lanterns. Connie sat on one of the ledges around the gallery, looking up at the dome as the verger talked, her face intent. Her head rested against the wall.

A grin spread over Will's face. He'd been brought here as a boy, and subjected to a similar lecture about the building. He'd forgotten almost all he'd been told, but there was one fact he and Alfred had remembered.

He sat on the ledge himself. There was no-one else in the gallery at the moment, and the verger was facing Connie, well away from the wall.

"Connie," he whispered, his cheek resting against the stone. Then again.

She turned her head slightly.

"Connie."

This time she looked at him, puzzlement clear on her face. The verger followed her gaze.

"The gallery also has interesting acoustic properties, my lady," he said, loudly enough for Will to hear.

"I love you," he whispered, in the pause before the verger spoke again, and a blush spread across her cheeks. She flapped a hand at him, and stood up, out of range of more whispers. But she did say something to the verger, and he saw something change hands before the man bowed and took himself off. He watched the sway of her hips as she walked around the gallery towards him.

"Sorry, Will, we have been here rather a long time."

"We can come again," he said. "Have you nothing to say to me in return?"

She took his arm, a seductive smile on her face. "No. I thought I'd take you home and show you instead."

The End

AFTERWORD

Thank you for reading *A Winning Trick*; I hope you enjoyed it. If you also enjoyed reading *Sauce for the Gander*, please could you leave a review for that on Amazon? You only need to write a few words. Reviews really help authors to get more readers.

My newsletters will let you know about new releases or special offers. I promise not to bombard you with emails. If you're not already signed up, you can do so via my website. The website also has details about forthcoming books, and links to my Facebook, Twitter, and Pinterest pages.

Website: www. jaynedavisromance.co.uk

Facebook: www.facebook.com/jaynedavisromance

Twitter: twitter.com/jaynedavis142

Pinterest: www.pinterest.co.uk/jaynedavis142

THE MRS MACKINNONS

England, 1799

Major Matthew Southam returns from India, hoping to put the trauma of war behind him and forget his past. Instead, he finds a derelict estate and a family who wish he'd died abroad.

Charlotte MacKinnon married without love to avoid her father's unpleasant choice of husband. Now a widow with a young son, she lives in a small Cotswold village with only the money she earns by her writing.

Matthew is haunted by his past, and Charlotte is fearful of her father's renewed meddling in her future. After a disastrous first meeting, can they help each other find happiness?

Available from Amazon on Kindle and in paperback. Read free in Kindle Unlimited. Listen via Audible, audiobooks.com, or other retailers.

AN EMBROIDERED SPOON

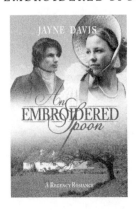

Wales 1817

After refusing every offer of marriage that comes her way, Isolde Farrington is packed off to a spinster aunt in Wales until she comes to her senses.

Rhys Williams, there on business, is turning over his uncle's choice of bride for him, and the last thing he needs is to fall for an impertinent miss like Izzy – who takes Rhys for a yokel.

Izzy's new surroundings make her look at life, and Rhys, afresh. But when her father, Lord Bedley, discovers that the situation in Wales is not what he thought, and that Rhys is in trade, a gulf opens for a pair who've come to love each other.

Will a difference in class keep them apart?

Available from Amazon on Kindle and in paperback (normal and Large Print). Read free in Kindle Unlimited.

CAPTAIN KEMPTON'S CHRISTMAS

A 100 page novella.

Lieutenant Philip Kempton and Anna Tremayne fall in love during one idyllic summer fortnight. When he's summoned to rejoin his ship, Anna promises to wait for him.

While he's at sea, she marries someone else.

Now she's widowed and he's Captain Kempton. When they meet again, can they put aside betrayal and rekindle their love?

Available from Amazon on Kindle and in paperback. Read free in Kindle Unlimited.

ABOUT THE AUTHOR

I wanted to be a writer when I was in my teens, hooked on Jane Austen and Georgette Heyer (and lots of other authors). Real life intervened, and I had several careers, including as a non-fiction author under another name. That wasn't *quite* the writing career I had in mind, but finally I am writing historical romance.

www.jaynedavisromance.co.uk

Printed in Great Britain
by Amazon